DREAM BECOME NIGHTMARE

"A people must always have a dream, Ian Lacklin. And I gave them the Dream—that we would increase in number and return one day to the paradise that had been fouled by those who are not of our blood. And we would purge the Earth of its filth. We would take our revenge for the Blooding Time.

"And you, Ian Lacklin, you gave me the means of our return. Your ship's computer tells me your people are weak. We have searched a millennium to transcend light-speed, and to think that its discovery would be a mere accident by an amateur back on Earth. And now your ship's computer tells *me* how. I shall lead in glory as my people return to paradise!"

INTO THE SEA OF STARS

William R. Forstchen

A Del Rey Book

BALLANTINE BOOKS • NEW YORK

PROLOGUE

It was a time of high adventure; an age when men and women could seize destiny and shape it to their will. Can our generation again breed such heroes? I think not, for a golden age of exploration comes but rarely to a race, and ours is now lost forever. They were of the same mold as Alexander at the Asian Gate and Caesar at the Rubicon.

Look to the choices that lay before them, a thousand years ago in the darkness of the twenty-first century. The world beneath them was poised for the madness of thermonuclear night; a madness that threatened to reach out to the Earth's thousand colonies. And with that madness came the calling—the calling from Old America, and Europe, and the vast reaches of the Asian giants. A calling for the children to return, to arm themselves, and to join in the war of the parent states. A war that would engulf mankind and create another dark age, from which we have so recently emerged.

But the colonies were no longer of Earth. They were

the new children, those who beheld a new horizon and could look beyond the parochial squabblings below.

And one day they were gone. Pointing their colonies into the unknown, they abandoned Earth forever. Using plasma drives, ion thrusters, matter/antimatter engines, thermonuclear pulse propulsion, and even solar sails, the colonies broke the bonds and headed off into the un-known—looking for freedom and an escape. Led by such legendary men as Ikawa Kurosawa, Vasiliy Renikoff, and Franklin Smith, the colonies abandoned the parent world to its madness. And then the War came.

Where are they now? What great wonders have these visionaries of the past created, unhindered by the Holo-caust War of the twenty-first century and the chaos that followed? Will we ever know the fate of the colonies missing for a thousand years?

From a rejected manuscript by Dr. Ian Lacklin, *Missing Colonies and the Heroic Figure in History.*

CHAPTER 1

"MR. HANSIN, ARE YOU WITH US, OR ARE YOU AGAIN PON-dering the earthly delights awaiting you in the women's dormitory?" In disgust Ian Lacklin collapsed into his chair and awaited the response.

"Ah, oh yes, I fully agree with you, Dr. Lacklin. Of course, you're absolutely right."

An undercurrent of snickers ran through the stuffy, overcrowded room. Ian stared them down and was greeted with forced looks of attentiveness.

Idiots. Graduate students, indeed. Every semester he was lectured by the dean that this year's was the best crop yet, survivors of a lengthy winnowing process. The dean made Kutzburg sound like Nouveau Harvard instead of the Provincial University's worst campus, one that ca-tered to ozone-head athletes and near-morons who had failed entry in every other system and, therefore, would become educators.

"Then, Mr. Hansin, perhaps you could enlighten us all

as to the ramifications of the Geosync Positions Communications Treaty of 2031 and how it was later cited by Beaulieu as the underlying cause of the Second South American Crisis of 2038."

"Say, Dr. Lacklin, was that in our readings?"

"By God, man, yes!" In exasperation Ian rose up to his full five-and-a-half-foot height and pointed a stubby finger at Hansen.

"Can't you see how important this was? With the crowding of the geosync points in the early part of the twenty-first century came the increasing agitation by the equatorial countries for control not only of the atmosphere above them but of the geosync positions, as well. Out of *that* came the abortive attempt to take Powersat 23 from the Sino-Japanese Energy Consortium, which in turn placed in jeopardy the Skyhook construction project in Malaysia. Can't you see how important that is to your life today?"

Blank stares greeted him. An ocean of blank stares.

"This room is a vacuum!" Ian shouted, waving his short, pudgy arms. "I know this course is required. I know you were all dragged in here kicking and screaming, but, by God, it's required for a reason.

"But, of course, you cretins already know that when you are history teachers yourselves, instructions in throwing a ball through a hoop will be far more important than this." Ian realized that his sarcasm was lost on that crowd, but with a note of pleading in his voice he valiantly tried to push ahead. "Don't you realize that you should also be able to teach your students about history, as well? Can't you see that?"

"Sure, Doc. We see that, but it's Friday, and the shuttle tram's leaving for Bostem in half an hour."

"Ah, a visit to the fleshpots of Bostem is more important to you than this, is that it, Mr. Hansin? And you, too, Mr. Roy?"

Silence.

"Well, Mr. Roy, don't sit there slack-jawed and drooling, answer me."

"Doc, that's an interesting point, and most difficult to answer."

Ian's cherubic face turned crimson. "Idiots, get out, just get out of here." His voice cracked on a high note, as it always did when he got excited. "Just get out!"

The mindless herd of thirty-odd students exploded into action and stampeded past him for the doorway.

"Wait, wait a minute, your reading assignment for next week..." But they were already gone, the corridor echoing with the sounds of their cattlelike trampling and muted comments about Lacklin's heritage and physiological shortcomings.

Another brilliant lecture wasted. Mumbling obscure Old American obscenities, he returned to his desk and started to shuffle a pile of notes into his briefcase. Eighteen years! Eighteen years of trying to give to an uncaring mob a brief glimpse of the joys to be found in history. There was an occasional pearl to be found, but for most of them, he was "Lackless Lacklin," master of "Enrichment Requirement Number 3: Sputnik to Armageddon— a History of the First Space Era."

"Excuse me, Dr. Lacklin."

"Yes, yes, what is it?" He looked up from his desk. "What is it, Shelley, why weren't you sucked into the vortex of that mob?"

"You were about to give an assignment?"

He looked at her appraisingly, the pearl of the semester, a gangly six-foot, twenty-one-year old; suffering from a bad case of acne and allegedly responsible to him as a research assistant—assigned by the dean, no doubt, as a practical joke. As a graduate student she was adequate, but she constantly hung around his office looking for sophomoric debates on the real meaning of Lock's theories of space sociology or other such foolishness.

"Do we have an assignment in Beaulieu's book?" she asked eagerly.

"No doubt, you've already finished it?"

"Of course, but I wanted to be ready for Monday's class. I can review it over the weekend."

"Don't worry about it now, why don't you just go along with the others."

"Here, let me help you back to the office with that." Before he could object, Shelley picked up the model of the Schuder space colony and started for the door.

"Damn it, look out!"

But it was too late. She brushed against the doorway, knocking the antennae structure off.

"Oh, Dr. Lacklin, I'm sorry, I—"

"Never mind, Miss Walker, just take it down to the office."

With a sigh of despair he picked up the broken plastic and followed after her. It had taken him the better part of a weekend to construct the three-foot-long model of a colony that had once been home to fifty thousand people.

As they made their way down the dimly lit corridors to Ian's subterranean office, Shelley chattered on about a paper she was writing for *The Journal of Space Antiquities*, and Dr. Lacklin occasionally grunted noncommittally, but his thoughts were already light-years away.

A new copy of the journal had just come that morning, with a lengthy article by Beaulieu concerning the recently discovered ruins of the colony on Mars. The site was one of the biggest finds of the decade and was revealing a wealth of artifacts on early twenty-first-century technology. The article would provide an excellent weekend's entertainment away from students, the school, the world— in fact, an escape from *all* reality.

Ian was so wrapped in happy thoughts of escape that he didn't notice Shelley had stopped, and Ian crashed right into her. The Schuder model tumbled to the floor and fractured into fragments that went spinning out in every direction.

"Uh-oh," Shelley whispered.

"Damn it, Shelley, why can't you . . . ?" Ian looked past her and saw the towering figure standing by the doorway to his office.

"It's Chancellor Cushman," Shelley whispered fearfully.

The figure started to move toward them. "Dr. Lacklin, my good man," the Chancellor's voice boomed like a cannon report, "just the person I was looking for."

Striding forward, hand outstretched, he stepped on broken fragments of the model, grinding them to powder. Grabbing Ian's shoulder, the Chancellor smiled his sinister toothy grin, which more often than not was the opening signal for a budget cut or an increase in one's teaching load.

He turned to Shelley with that same grin, but there was a barely concealed disdain about him as he was forced to address a student. "My charming young miss, would you be so kind as to excuse the good doctor and me."

Before the Chancellor had finished speaking, Shelley was backing away, mumbling something about having to wash her hair; she was gone, leaving Ian to his fate.

Ian followed the Chancellor down the corridor into the dusty, cluttered closet that was Ian's office. There the Chancellor released his numbing grip on Ian's shoulder. He ran his finger along a bookcase and snorted with disdain when the digit came up black with two decades' worth of dust. Walking around to Ian's desk, the Chancellor first carefully examined the chair as if expecting it to be booby-trapped, and then, barely satisfied, he lowered his towering form while pointing Ian to the visitor's chair on the other side of the desk.

"You know, Ian," his voice boomed, filling the tiny room, "I never could see the purpose of keeping your history program alive. Such things are a waste, in my mind." He smiled.

It's termination! Ian thought. My God, what will I do?

"But the Provincial Government of New America," the Chancellor continued, "decreed in the educational charter to this institution that we are to, quote, 'train functioning citizens who shall fit into the framework of our society and appreciate the traditions of our new Federated Republic,' unquote. In other words, my man, we are to train effective cogs for the wheels of the administration. And one of the teeth in that cog must be an understanding of history. Do you agree?"

Maybe it's not termination! "Of course, your Excellency, of course." His voice cracked.

"I knew you would agree, my good man. Of course, I've always felt that such courses as File Management or Interoffice Communications were far more valuable than your digging up the ancient past, but this is an institute of higher learning so we must be tolerant of minor eccentricities, mustn't we?"

"Of course."

"Tell me, Ian, how many people staff your department now?"

"I'm the only one. Don't you remember you cut the budget last year, eliminating Mr. Lelezi?"

"Ah, yes. Mr. Lelezi. He taught the history of the Holocaust War and the Second Dark Age?"

"Yes, your Excellency."

"The taped lectures we've made of him are an adequate replacement, are they not? Save us a significant sum, don't they?"

It would be termination!

"Tell me, Ian, do we have tapes of your lectures on file?"

Ian could only nod. The Chancellor had instituted that little trick five years back. The Board of Regents loved it, and the Chancellor was now hailed as a bold new innovator in education.

"Good, Dr. Lacklin, very good indeed. Would you be so kind as to write up a study guide for your course, in triplicate, and be sure to use the proper forms. I want it in my office first thing Monday morning."

The room started to spin. Ian felt as if he were looking up from the bottom of a deep, deep well, and the only thing he could see at the end of the shaft was the Chancellor's wolfish grin.

"Does this mean," Ian asked weakly, trying to conceal the wheedling tone in his voice, "that my position is to be automated?"

"Well, my good man"—the Chancellor laughed, obviously delighting in this little diversion—"don't be so pale and glum. You don't want to spend the rest of your life in a classroom, now do you?"

"But history is my life, it's everything."

The Chancellor's grin suddenly became more sinister. "We've other plans for you."

"Other plans?"

"Come now, Ian, you now as well as I do that this noble institution supports its staff and encourages it to broaden the field of knowledge through publication. I've been checking on you, my man—in eighteen years of teaching, you've never been published."

"There is my book, you know! *Missing Colonies and the Heroic Figure in History*."

"How many rejections have you had on that?"

Ian was silent.

"But that's not what I'm talking about. There are other forms of writing, take grants, for instance."

He wants me as a grant writer! Endless forms to fill out. I'll go mad, Ian thought. Digging the sands of Mars would be better. Perhaps Beaulieu would take me on as an assistant. But his stomach turned somersaults at the mere thought of space travel and weightlessness.

"You have some rather good experience with grants, my man. In fact, that's the reason for this friendly chat of ours. It's your grant, Ian. I just got a call from the Minister of Education, who has a brother in the Deep Space Exploration and Surveying Department. I'm talking about your grant proposal."

"My grant proposal?" I've never written a grant proposal. Ian was about to say that he had no idea what the Chancellor was talking about, but then thought it might be better not to admit such ignorance.

"You do remember your grant proposal?" the Chancellor asked suspiciously.

Ian forced a smile and nodded noncommittally.

"Right, then. I just wanted to be the first to congratulate you. Your grant has come through. You know what this means for our school? Isn't this wonderful?"

"It's come through," Ian replied, trying to keep his confusion out of his voice. "Why, that's wonderful." What the hell is he talking about?

"Well, aren't you excited, my good man? Think of the prestige it will bring to this institution."

And to your plans for being the next Minister of Education, Ian thought.

"Don't you have anything to say?"

Ian could only smile weakly.

"Ah, I understand, of course you're in shock over this whole thing. But you'd better get cracking, my good man. You're to be out of here Tuesday morning. By the way, are your passport and twenty-three–forty-four medical form up to date?"

"My twenty-three–forty-four?"

A glint of suspicion appeared in the Chancellor's eyes. He examined Ian as if he were an insect under a magnifying glass.

"Wake up, man, wake up. Your twenty-three–forty-four!"

"Sir, what is a twenty-three–forty-four?" Ian bleated.

"Good God, man, don't you understand what I'm talking about?" Exasperated, the Chancellor opened his attaché case and pulled out a heavy document, bound in a red jacket. There was a quick flurry of pages and the Chancellor started to read.

"'All members of the party must qualify for translight travel by successfully undergoing a full twenty-three—forty-four medical review.' Dr. Lacklin, you wrote that in the grant proposal, or don't you remember? It's standard medical policy for anyone traveling aboard the new translight vessels."

"I'm traveling translight!" Ian shouted in terror.

The Chancellor stood up to his full six-and-a-half-foot height and advanced around the desk. He loomed over Ian as if he were closing in for the kill, and Ian slipped lower into his seat.

"Dr. Lacklin, do you understand anything at all concerning what we've been talking about?"

Ian tried to sound self-assured, but only a mousy "no" squeaked out of him.

A forefinger was suddenly pointed into Ian's chest and with each word spoken the Chancellor stabbed at Ian with such force that Ian feared a rib might be broken.

"Dr. Lacklin, at the beginning of this semester a grant proposal left the history department under your signature. *Your* department, and *your* signature, Dr. Lacklin. And this document was addressed to the Department of Deep Space Survey and Exploration. Last year the DSSE announced that an Alpha 3 translight survey ship would be released from active service and placed at the disposal of the Ministry of Education, and grant proposals would be accepted as to its implementation and use. Do you follow me so far, Dr. Lacklin?"

"Yes."

"You are aware, of course, Dr. Lacklin, that we have only returned to space within the last hundred years and that translight was only discovered within the last fifteen years. I am sure, Dr. Lacklin, that you realize that there are only eleven translight ships available, and the Alpha 3 is the first such model."

"Yes, I am a professor of space history," Ian replied, trying to sound insulted over such a simple question.

"Good. I wasn't sure on that point." The Chancellor cut him an icy gaze.

"The Alpha 3 was to be retired," Ian interjected. "The damn thing is unsafe; all the other ships of the same design have never returned."

"Not to worry." And the Chancellor laughed. "I've been assured that little problem has been cleared up. But as I was telling you, Dr. Lacklin, the grant proposal under your signature requested use of that vehicle and, I quote, 'to attempt reestablishment of contact with the seven hundred colonies that abandoned near-Earth space on the eve of the Holocaust War. This will be accomplished by consulting those surviving records, recently uncovered, which indicate the courses of the colonies. Using translight propulsion it will be a simple matter of following the original courses and thus overtaking the units,' unquote."

The Chancellor fixed Ian with a deadly, penetrating gaze. "Dr. Lacklin, did you write this grant proposal?"

Ian looked up and started to answer.

"The truth, Dr. Lacklin, or you'll regret it!"

"No." His answer came out as a timid squeak.

In exasperation the Chancellor slammed the proposal onto Ian's desk. A flurry of dust swirled around the two men. The Chancellor suddenly reached across the table, grabbed hold of the proposal, and threw it into Ian's lap.

"Then look at this, damn it!"

Ian picked it up and, adjusting his glasses, he peered owllike at the cover.

"'A proposal for the implementation of the Alpha 3 unit for the reestablishment of contact with colonial units

of the twenty-first century, submitted by Dr. Ian Lacklin,
Provincial University System.'"

Ian suddenly felt very sick.

He pulled open the proposal and started to scan it.

"Turn to the last page, damn you!"

Ian obeyed the shouted command.

Proposed Crewing of the Alpha 3 *Discovery*

Understanding the extreme limitation on crew space
and taking into consideration the isolation from
any higher authority, it should be realized that the
crew must deal with all contingencies related to
establishing contact with human colonies while
out of contact with Earth. Crew proposal is as
follows:

1. Pilot of the Alpha 3 unit with previous experience in deep space flight and isolation.

2. Medical/biological technician with an understanding of medical situations unique to the twenty-
first century, since all units contacted will have been
isolated with their particular varieties of microbes
for the last 1107 years.

3. Sociological/psychological personnel capable
of dealing with the ramifications of cross-cultural
exposure and shock.

4. Assistant to the program director, capable of
logging all reports, administering to all reporting,
filing, and data management.

5. Program director, versed in twenty-first-
century history, in particular relating to all aspects
of the establishment of the self-contained colonies
starting in 2019 until the decision to flee near-Earth
space in the year 2078. The program director must
be familiar with each of the colonial units in question, their engineering, sociological backgrounds,
cultural makeup, and administrative organizations.

Sweat broke out on Ian's forehead. He stopped for a moment to look up at the Chancellor and was met with a glacial stare. He returned to his reading.

The program director should have a full understanding of the process leading to the decision by
the seven hundred colonial units to abandon Earth
on the eve of the Holocaust War. The program director should be familiar with the trajectories selected by the units when evacuating near-Earth space
and have reasonable estimates of distance traveled
by each unit since departure. All such data is currently on file with the author and is available upon
request.

Ian groaned softly and looked up imploringly at the Chancellor.

"Look at that signature," the Chancellor hissed.

Ian did as ordered and stared numbly at the signature and personal seal placed upon the last page of the proposal. They were his, all right.

"Can you explain this?!" the Chancellor demanded.

Ian could only shake his head.

"Are those your signature and personal seal?"

"Yes," he replied weakly.

"Then, good God, man, this is your grant proposal!"

"But I didn't write it."

"Oh, yes you did, Dr. Lacklin, you most certainly did. My contact over at the Ministry has informed me that the grant has been approved and that the decision has already been made that you, as the author of this grant, shall lead the mission.

"Dr. Lacklin, I don't give a good damn if you wrote this thing or not, but as far as anyone is now concerned, you are the sole author of it and will take responsibility as mission head. I'll not have it said that this document got past my office and then turned out to be a fake. I'd be the laughingstock of the profession. Dr. Lacklin, this one is yours and you are going for a ride with it!"

"I can't!"

"What do you mean, you can't? I don't think I'm hearing you correctly."

"You know and I know that those Alpha 3s never came back. Besides, I get deathly sick anytime I travel."

In his panic he could already conjure up a hundred possible deaths in the mad venture—they could have an engine overload, or misnavigation could send them into a black hole. And the quarters, they were so cramped the claustrophobia alone would kill him. He wasn't going out there, and that was that. He was a historian, a dealer in the safeness of the past—not some crazed adventurer. He simply reported and glorified it all. It sure as hell wasn't his job to go out and actually do it.

The Chancellor settled back in his chair and with a sudden change of tack started to smile gently. "Come, come, Dr. Lacklin, think of the opportunity. This is your field. Think of the lucrative offers upon your return. By heavens, man, the publishers would even snatch up that book you're working on."

"I can't go. I'm afraid of flying."

"Dr. Lacklin, think how ridiculous we'd look if it suddenly came out that you were not the author of this grant."

"I don't care if I look ridiculous."

"But I care, Dr. Lacklin. I most certainly care." There was a note of threat in the voice that carried a distinct warning.

"Look, Ian"—and the Chancellor leaned forward, trying to put on the suave charm though it was obvious that near-homicidal rage churned just below the surface—"I'll make it as plain as can be. This will put our university on the map. And it will be one of my department people who did it. The regional board of directors will take very favorable notice of a campus with such a success."

"And over my vaporized body, you'll move into the National Bureau of Education," Ian muttered.

"What was that?"

"Oh, nothing, your Excellency, nothing."

"Then you'll still refuse to take responsibility for this grant and will refuse the position of project manager?"

Ian didn't answer.

"You'll be the coward just because of a little physical discomfort and a very slight risk of danger?"

Ian could only nod his head.

"All right then, if that's the way you want it." The Chancellor suddenly turned and started for the door.

Ian slumped back into his chair and breathed an audible sigh of relief. He knew a terrible revenge would be exacted for his refusal, but anything was better than going "out there."

The Chancellor started to open the door and then turned, giving Ian a cold-blooded look of appraisal. "By the way, Dr. Lacklin. Have you ever heard of a young coed named Makena LaFay?"

Panic seized Ian's face. Cushman knew he had hit the right lever.

"Well, have you?"

"Yes." The answer was barely a whisper.

"She's the daughter of the provincial Governor, you know. I've met Jeremiah LaFay any number of times. His support of the Reform Puritanical Movement is well known.

"I'd never want to cross him myself—his ability to have opponents and personal enemies arrested for, how shall I say, 'alleged violations of public morals' is well known."

Ian appeared to be on the edge of cardiac arrest.

"Of course, I know dear Makena was an aggressive young lady," the Chancellor continued with a cold, malicious grin, "who perhaps did not live up to her father's personal code of morality. In fact, one of my informants in the women's living quarters stated that when Makena was a student last semester she openly boasted, 'I twisted an A out of that fat little fool with only one night in the sack.' Do you know who that fat little fool is, Dr. Lacklin?"

A groan escaped from Ian. He couldn't help what had happened. She had been waiting for him at his apartment in a state of extreme undress, giving full exposure to her ample charms. He had tried valiantly to show her the door, but in the end, simple human nature won out. After all, it had been several years since . . .

"But I only gave her a B."

"Ah, *only* a B. Only a *B*! So, you don't deny it!"

Ian shrugged his shoulders.

"Well, my good man, I know about this little B. In fact, half the females on this campus know about that little B. And with a single phone call I can arrange for our good friend the Governor to know about that little B! And then we'll all get to see 'Only a B' Lacklin get his butt end hauled off by some of LaFay's gorillas, who would love to smash you to a pulp for violating the innocence of our good Governor's virginal daughter."

"Virginal! She attacked me, your Excellency, I didn't stand a chance."

"Ah, so you admit it, then. Frankly, Ian, I find that impossible to accept. In the eyes of our good God-fearing Governor, his Little Precious is purer than arctic snow. It would break my heart to have to tell him that she had been brutally violated by one of my staff, who, of course, has just been fired."

The Chancellor started to smile again. "But never fear, good friend. Of course I could never do that to the hero of Kutzburg Provincial. Of course not. I think this little matter can be forgotten for someone with your stature. Now, my friend, I do believe we understand each other."

Ian nodded dumbly. There was a seventy-five percent chance of a quick death in space. But he knew there would be a hundred percent chance of a couple of broken arms, and God knows what else, if he stayed.

"Fine, then, just fine, and let me be the first to offer you my congratulations. I'll send the necessary paperwork down this afternoon and the school physician will be by within the hour to start processing your twenty-three—forty-four. If I might be so bold, I'll help you out with assigning your medical person and sociologist, and you can have the liberty of appointing your administrative assistant. Have a pleasant day, Dr. Lacklin. And I'll expect you in my office at nine sharp Monday morning."

The Chancellor closed the door behind him and started off for the Academic Records Office. There was a little question of a grade change up to an A that had to be looked into. After all, he had promised her he would take care of it. And just to make sure there wasn't an embarrassing change of heart, he would push Ian off-planet within the week, along with the other embarrassing clowns on his staff. He could already picture his new office in the National Bureau. He smiled in anticipation.

Ian tried to control the wild panic and for a moment he contemplated suicide. But that required a little more courage than he could muster, and he pushed the thought aside; the reams of work facing him that weekend would require some help. He'd better give Shelley a call.

Shelley! He leaped out of his chair and pulled open the door. And there she was. As if waiting for him.

"Dr. Lacklin, ah, yeah. Ah, I thought I, ah, left my books here..."

Once a week Shelley took him a pile of paperwork. It got so that he never even bothered to ask what the individual items where, and he merely signed each document or memo and affixed his personal seal to it. The damn woman had written the grant and sneaked it in with the other paperwork, since only a fully accredited instructor could make grant applications to the Ministry.

"Get in here!" Ian shouted, suddenly finding a way at last to vent his frustration.

"Ah, well, you see, Doctor. I, ah, got this book I want to read. Couldn't I, ah—"

"If you value your life, you better get your butt in here right now!"

CHAPTER 2

Brazil's tropical heat was finally locked out by the silent closing of the liftcar's door. Ian gratefully sank into the first available seat and Shelley eased in alongside. Mopping his face with a soaked handkerchief, Ian breathed a sigh of relief as the frigid air washed over him. The air-conditioning in the Brasilia Skyhook Station was again down for "routine inspection," meaning that the incompetent ground staff would take two weeks to find out what was wrong. The result had been an agonizing eight hours of 100-degree heat while waiting for the next liftcar. Now that his fear of dying from the heat was removed, Ian Lacklin again had time to curse the fates in general and Chancellor Cushman in particular.

After the initial shock of the Chancellor's news had worn off, Ian had thought that, bureaucrats being what they are, it would take a year at the very least before the mission was cleared for launch. Given that much time, he had naively reasoned there would be ample opportunities to gum up the paperwork into such a tangle that the mission would just keep getting delayed, postponing forever the dreaded jump into deep space.

But he now realized that the Chancellor had been half a dozen moves ahead of him from the beginning. Ian's battle plan collapsed in a paper blizzard as the Chancellor outclassed and outmaneuvered him in every bureaucratic strategem possible.

In the final act of a "team spirit send-off," the Chancellor had personally driven Ian and Shelley to the New Bostem airstrip for their connecting flight to the Brasilia Skyhook Station. Shelley and the Chancellor had even managed to have a fairly civil conversation about the prospects before them. As a final gesture he gave them a send-off bouquet of flowers, which made Ian sneeze.

Ian turned in his seat and gave Shelley an appraising glance. Why he had requested her was beyond him. Perhaps it was revenge for her getting him into the mess. He knew he wasn't attracted to her in any physical way; she was all adolescent angles, even though she was already in her early twenties. She had the air typical of a studious female, one who would forever be bound to a book, wear the most uncomplimentary of heavy wools, and never be cured of near-terminal acne.

If Shelley had any positive feature, it was her ability to cover his tail when it came to paperwork and organization. Only Shelley could make any sense out of Ian's data files—if Ian had to run up his data by himself he would soon be totally lost ... Ian's contemplation of Shelley ended as the liftcraft attendant turned on the information channel.

"Welcome to Brasilia Station, Skyhook 4. Your liftcraft is now preparing for departure."

Shelley turned to Ian with a bewildered look and he realized that her chair speaker was set for Portuguese. Turning the switch on her armrest to English, he settled back and tried to calm his nerves.

"We apologize for any inconvenience you may have suffered because of the malfunctioning air-conditioning system. Now that you are aboard the liftcraft you may rest assured that our crew will see to your every comfort."

Some of the hundred-odd passengers laughed, but their biting comments about the competence of the staff and the safety of the liftcraft didn't help Ian in the slightest.

"Our transit time to Geosync Station 4 will be eleven hours and twenty minutes . . ." The voice droned on about emergency procedures and safety regulations, but Ian's thoughts had already drifted away.

The liftcar started to shake, and Shelley's hand dug into his forearm. "What was that?" she whispered hoarsely.

Ian pointed out the window and smiled at her as if she were a naive child.

"Why, we've started up, that's all."

The car silently started its ascent up the vertical track, exerting a slight pressure in the pit of his stomach. Suddenly they cleared the interior of the Brasilia station and broke into the tropical sunlight. Their speed was already better than a kilometer a minute and the ground dropped away.

How undramatic this all is, Ian thought sadly, even though he fully realized that he would have been terrified by the old way of trans-Earth lift-off. The days of chemical rockets belching scarlet plumes of incandescent flame were gone forever. Never would he have the chance to go roaring into the heavens atop a crackling, thundering throne of fire. That was gone, long since gone—a distant memory already half a hundred years past, now that the Skyhook Towers girdled the equator with a ring of spokes. The towers rose tens of thousands of kilometers to geosync and yet that distance beyond for the necessary counterweighting. The trip into space was reduced to a simple elevator ride; a very long elevator ride, to be sure, but lacking the thundering grandeur of so long ago.

Shelley was quickly glued to the window as they rose

up and away. At the twenty-kilometer level the curvature of the Earth was ever so slightly visible, and Ian could see the deepening indigo of their destination. Pressing up against the window alongside Shelley, he looked down on the Earth, which was dropping away with ever-increasing speed.

For long minutes Shelley stayed pressed to the window, until a faint groan sounded alongside her. "Dr. Lacklin, what's wrong?"

"Just thinking about zero G, that's all"—he moaned feebly—"just thinking about zero G." And he fumbled through the storage pouch alongside his chair, making sure that the white plastic bags were there, ready for his use.

The acceleration was light but constant, as if a gentle hand were pushing them back into their couches. Zero gravity would not occur until the car arrived at the geosync station, where their velocity in relationship to the Earth would cancel out their potential rate of fall.

But Ian attempted to divert his thoughts from that dreaded moment by looking out at the indigo band that marked the upper reaches of the Earth's atmosphere.

As if on cue, the steward appeared, pushing a cart laden with the more potent forms of liquid relaxant. Ian handed over a fiver, pointed with three fingers to a dark amber bottle, and an icy triple of rum was produced.

He settled back into his chair and took a long, refreshing sip. So he was embarking on the great journey, following the path of his heroes on their outward reach to the stars. How often he had tried to romanticize this to his bored students, who viewed the exploration of space with not one-tenth the interest that was reserved for the afternoon video love shows. How he longed for the world of a millennium earlier, when things were held in their proper perspective.

Idiots! At least I'm away from them. He took another swallow. In spite of his fears, Ian felt a tingling, a surge of excitement. He was reaching out along the same path that millions had followed so long ago. He would at last have the chance to follow them outward and discover the secret of their odyssey.

The thought set his heart to pounding. He was about to realize the ultimate fantasy of any good historian—to come face to face with the past. With luck he might even find a Mitsubishi Habitat, or one of the old O'Neill Cylinders. Ian knew historians who would joyfully have killed their mothers if it meant a chance to meet with Churchill or to witness the Mongol burning of Kiev. And here was his chance, his dream coming out to meet him. He could remember how Lelezi dreamed of finding a tape showing a Saturn V lift-off. Sure, once that would have given Ian a thrill, but now he was going for far bigger game.

The steward came by again and Ian waved for another triple. Shelley gave him a frown.

His mind lapsed into happy reverie. He could imagine meeting in secret with Smith and the Council of Ten as they made their momentous decision to abandon Earth on the eve of the Holocaust War. Yes, Ian Lacklin, announcing to a startled world the forming of the Alliance and the Declaration of Severance . . .

"It's wonderful, just simply wonderful!"

Several heads turned to look at him, but he didn't give a damn. Hell no, they can all kiss off. He was Ian Lacklin, noted historian, soon to be explorer. Why, damn it, once he returned from this voyage, there wouldn't be a publisher in the country crazy enough to turn down his manuscripts. He'd have it made. Yes sir, he could snap his fingers at the Chancellor, why, even the Governor could kiss his butt. The thought of such a thing made him laugh out loud. And to think that just a week ago he was terrified about the Governor's ever finding out about him and what's-her-name.

And the Chancellor, yeah the Chancellor. Good-bye to that rotten SOB and all the bureaucratic nightmares of teaching at a government-run institution. No more damned memos about using the correct forms, or inventories reporting how many erasers were missing, or asinine education courses. No sir, Ian thought, no more faculty meetings, and most of all, no more educational politics. "No more!" he shouted out loud. "Say, steward, get over here if you please, my good man."

Shelley was looking around the cabin in mortal embarrassment, when an insistent warning beeper suddenly kicked on. "All passengers, this is your flight director. Please be sure that your safety belts are fastened." Ian paid it no heed.

Shelley looked over at Ian and made sure that he was strapped in.

"We have reached maximum velocity; our acceleration will terminate in ten seconds. You'll experience a momentary sensation of lightness when acceleration cuts out. We know you'll enjoy it as a pleasant foretaste of zero G at Geosync 4. Thank you."

"And you know what I'd like to tell Miss Redding, Miss C.C. Set Procedures Redding right now?" Ian shouted.

Shelley looked at him wide-eyed. In her entire sheltered experience of university parents and honors dormitories, she had never been forced to deal with a drunken male.

She was still searching for an apt response when the acceleration cut off. Shelley suddenly felt as if she had been riding an elevator (which indeed she was) and the vehicle had slowed while she kept going. Her stomach felt as if it were climbing out her mouth.

And suddenly she no longer had to think of how to respond to Ian. Her only concern now was to find enough towels to start cleaning up her thoroughly besotten professor.

* * *

"Yes, Dr. Redding, of course."

He tried to back out of the cramped middle cabin, but the laws of zero G tricked him. His arms flailing like berserk windmill sails, Richard Croce spun across the room, slapped into the wall, then ricocheted back toward Ellen Redding, who didn't hesitate for one second with her high-speed outpouring of vitriolic abuse.

"Damn it, woman, help me." Richard groaned as he did a slow rolling dive straight at her bulging midsection.

Grabbing hold of a support railing, Ellen gently pulled herself out of Richard's dive-bomb approach. He drifted past her and smacked into the opposite wall of the cabin, this time face first, but his outstretched hands grabbed a padded rail and prevented another pinball-like trajectory.

"Now, Dr. Croce, if you've stopped your acrobatic display of zero-gravity ineptitude, I would like to summarize my argument."

"Damn it, Ellen, I can't do anything about it."

"Dr. Redding to you, Doctor Croce." There was a sarcastic edge to how she said Dr. Croce— as if the linking of the two words were somehow impossible.

"All right, Dr. Redding," Richard replied coldly, "I'll remember your title." The rest of the sentence started to form but he thought better of it. He viewed doctorates in sociology and collective psychology as having the same validity as a doctorate in physical education or school administration.

"Thank you"—she hesitated for a moment, and then smiled icily—"Doctor."

He took several deep breaths in a vain attempt to calm himself, then decided to start in again. "And another thing, Captain Leminski stated that our gross weight is a hundred and twenty kilos over." He eyed her bulging form sarcastically, and she started to color into a deeper shade of purple that went beyond the flaming red of her hair.

"I know where we can dump off that weight right now," she replied evenly.

"I don't see anything coming off your manifest."

"Because it doesn't need to."

"A hundred and fifty kilos of survey forms in *triplicate*! You call that necessary!" Richard shouted.

"Dr. Croce, I've already explained to you that I've been sent on this expedition by our Chancellor to gather important data. The best way for a sociologist and collective psychologist to gather information is through observation and survey."

"You don't even know if they'll be able to read the damn things. Did you get your precious forms translated into Old English or Japanese or Russian? Well, did you?"

"There is no need of that. I'm sure your good friend Ian will be able to translate for us."

The loathing she put into the word Ian was almost frightening in its intensity. The faculty battles between Ian Lacklin and Ellen Redding were near legend. Richard pitied poor Ian when he came aboard.

"Dr. Redding, I'm sure the Chancellor doesn't give a good damn about these so-called Lost Colonies. Personally, I think this whole charade is nothing more than a hairbrained move on the Chancellor's part to get rid of his most embarrassing tenured faculty."

"Now, Croce, you—"

"Dr. Croce, to you."

Boiling with anger, Ellen stumbled for a response, and Richard pushed on.

"If—and I say, *if*—we find these colonies, I think Ian will have more to do with his time than to translate your half-witted sociological surveys to a bunch of people who most likely won't want to be surveyed in the first place. Therefore, my dear doctor, I think it only logical that your damn bloody forms should be heaved out right now."

"If anything is to be heaved, it should be those ten cases of alleged surgical and sterilization equipment." A smug smile lit up her pudgy face, and she laughed maliciously. "Besides, Doctor, a half hour ago I managed to put one of those cases through the airlock."

"You bitch! Do you know how hard it was to get that gin up here!" His voice trailed off into incoherent screams. One-tenth of his liquor, gone! Three years for this damned mission, and only nine cases to see him through! Richard barely heard Leminski shout over the intercom about a ship's docking alongside as he launched himself through the air toward Ellen.

The hatch behind them opened. A green face peered through. "Oh, my God." Ian groaned.

"Ah, Ian, old friend," Richard shouted, as he drifted within striking distance of Ellen, "you're just in time to witness the effect of zero gravity on blubber."

"Why, you pickled sot—"

"Enough! I've had enough!" A wiry form in blue coveralls pushed through the doorway behind Ian.

"Ah, Ian," Richard said with sudden cheer, "meet our pilot and guide through the universe, Stasz Leminski."

Ian extended his hand, but Stasz ignored him.

"I have my orders," Stasz whispered in a sharp, hissing voice. His five-and-a-half-foot, hundred-pound frame seemed to be a coiled bundle of energy ready to explode in violent rage at any second.

"The problem is simple. We need to dump one hundred and twenty kilos. You must decide which one hundred and twenty kilos within twenty-three hours. Antimatter ignition sequencing will start in twenty-six hours. If by three hours before departure you have not dumped the excess mass, I will do it for you."

Grabbing hold of a handrail, he turned himself about as if getting set to leave.

"Ah, Leminski, I don't think you quite understand," Ellen Redding said. She spoke with the pedantic style typical of a professor addressing an idiot or a first-year university student.

"I understand perfectly, Miss Redding." He smiled a

tight wolfish grin as she stiffened to the form of address. "You see, Miss Redding, I am the craft pilot and engineer, therefore I am responsible for the function of this wreck which the Confederation has pawned off on you . . . well, never mind that. As I was saying, when it comes to the function of this vessel, I am in control."

Pushing off, he floated back down the corridor.

Ellen turned on Ian, who quailed at the sight of his old nemesis. But before she could speak, Stasz's voice drifted back to them. "By the way, Dr. Redding, I'm declaring that Croce's 'surgical supplies' are now part of my ship's maintenance stores, therefore they are not to be touched. Dr. Lacklin, I'd suggest that those damned forms get dumped right now. Heaven knows how I hate forms; in fact, I've already got eighty kilos' worth in the airlock." He laughed sardonically and disappeared into the forward control room.

Sensing an impending explosion, Richard pushed past Ellen and mumbled an excuse about checking his equipment. As he drifted by Ian, his nose wrinkled at the sour smell.

"Good luck, old boy," Richard whispered.

"If I'd known that she was going to be aboard, I'd have stayed home in spite of the Chancellor," Ian whispered in reply. "Writing grants would be heaven compared to this."

"I heard that, Ian."

Richard grabbed Shelley's arm and pushed her out the hatch, abandoning Ian to what Richard told her would be "a friendly Social Science Departmental Meeting."

The shouting between the two old rivals filled the ship until Stasz finally called it to halt and begged for a little sleep before departure.

CHAPTER 3

"I THOUGHT IT ESSENTIAL THAT WE ALL SIT DOWN TOGETHER before departure and briefly review what we can expect."

Ian was trying to speak with an authoritative voice, but it came out more as a strangled croak. He and Ellen Redding had had such a knock-down drag out over who was in control of the mission that he had actually shouted himself hoarse. He looked across at her and tried a wan smile, but from her response it must have looked to her to be a threatening grimace. Nevertheless she said nothing; his halfhearted threat to call the Chancellor and resign over her presence, for the moment at least, had been the lever to submission.

"Why we've been assigned is the Chancellor's decision and not mine. But I can see where, if anything, he wished to get rid of three tenured faculty and bring in his own people—and, Ellen, I'd think even you'd agree with that."

She nodded her head sadly. Most of the campus staff knew about the affair between Ellen and the Chancellor a dozen years back, when he was still the glad-handing, ever-smiling young hotshot assistant to the assistant vice president. Out of that had come the famous nickname "C.C." Redding, which most faculty could guess at but usually would not discuss with anyone less than a graduate student.

Leminski floated to one side of the table and looked vacantly off into space with a slightly bored expression of disdain.

Ian cleared his throat and tried to continue. "Stasz, are we in trim for flight weight?"

"Yeah, and one kilo under. Croce and me drained off an extra bottle of gin and just discharged it a little while ago."

Oh, great, Ian thought, Richard has a new drinking buddy. The pilot to whom we've entrusted our lives.

"All right then, we've got our ship, everything is loaded, and now we have to decide where to go."

Richard looked up at Ian. "What do you mean, where do we go? Why, I thought this expedition was to look for the Lost Colonies."

"It's not that simple," Ian said softly. "Shelley's grant request mentioned in general terms the seven hundred lost colonies, and indeed if all of them survived, which is highly unlikely, we are now presented with an interesting piece of math which our dear sponsors never grasped."

"Go on," Ellen said softly, without a trace of anger. When it came to questions of odds and statistics, she was all professional and, in fact, even cordial.

"All right, here is what we know—the givens, so to speak. Starting in the year 2079 the first colonial units came to the decision to abandon Earth in light of the coming war. Their propulsion systems were stationkeeping units, not heavy-lift devices. Given the tech level of the period, the only propulsion units available were ion

drive, plasma drive, solar sail, antimatter, and thermonuclear pulse.

"Within four years the first unit completed its modi-
fications and was away. Seven hundred and twenty-three
departed before August 7, 2087, when the first wave of
EMP detonations on Earth and the subsequent strikes
wiped out all communication."

Ian was really getting into form now, and for once he
had an interested audience. His was no longer dry history—it was the information that would be the center of
their lives for the next three years.

"Could more units have left afterward?" Richard asked.

"Possibly. And just that question shows the problems
of this quest. There is only one absolute given in this
whole scheme. Six hundred and twelve units did pull out
of near-Earth orbit and one hundred and eleven others
pulled out from various deep-space orbits, including three
asteroid mining-survey colonies.

"But the data stops the day the war started, when the
tracking facilities on the Moon and Mars were knocked
out. So there is the potential that approximately seven
hundred other units, which were preparing to abandon
Earth orbit, did indeed abandon orbit."

"So that increases our odds tremendously?" Ellen asked
cautiously.

"Yes, from next to impossible to almost next to impossible. And I'm not being sarcastic. You see, the Copernicus site did have the initial trajectory data. In fact,
for the units that left several years before the war, the
data are pretty darn good, since they had time to do some
pinpoint tracking.

"So here we have the raw data of seven hundred-odd
colonies to start with, that's great. However, did you ever
stop to think"—and Ian was talking in general, but everyone could sense that it was directed toward Shelley—
"just how big it is out there?"

She smiled wanly and nodded. The stares of the other

three focused on her, and she could feel the hostility growing as each one thought about the fact that it was the overzealous young student who had pulled them from their more-comfortable niches and sent them to synchronous orbit.

"It's not that bad," she said meekly.

"Not that bad!" Stasz interjected. "My hand to God, for I speak the truth, it's merely numbing in size.

"How far could they have gone?" he asked, shifting his gaze from Shelley back to Ian.

"Not far. It's estimated that their drive systems at best could take them up to point-one light. Therefore, a maximum of 112 light-years out. That gives us a cubic volume of . . . let me see."

"Nearly ten million cubic light years." Ellen said softly, obviously proud that she could outdo them all in a little exercise of mental calculation.

"Therefore," Ian responded, "I present our problem— where do we start? We shall be looking for approximately seven hundred units in an area of ten million cubic light-years."

"Can't we eliminate a good part of that?" Richard asked.

"I think so," Stasz interjected. "The fifteen stars nearest to Earth have already been checked out—without any sign of refugee colonies. That eliminates nearly a hundred craft right there, since their trajectories carried them that way. Now, it is of course possible that they went to those systems, slingshoted around them, and went off on tangent trajectories, thereby making predictions of their whereabouts more difficult."

"And I think we can also eliminate two hundred or so colonies because the data we have on them indicates that they would not have survived the journey for long."

"Why so, Dr. Lacklin?" Shelley asked, curiosity overcoming her desire to hide.

"The answer is simple. We are dealing with closed ecosystems. There is a certain amount of free hydrogen available in interstellar space, and if you could accelerate up to ramjet velocities that would be useful, but outside of the propulsion systems, the colonies had to be one hundred percent closed."

"I'm not sure that I follow you," Ellen admitted.

"Well, let us say that a colony had a ninety-nine point nine percent reclamation rate for all combinations of oxygen. Let's say that across a time period of X, point one percent of the total oxygen supply is lost due to faulty reclamation, leaks, and such. Now, point one is not bad for any vessel if X equals one year. But look at the simple math—in one thousand years, unless another oxygen supply was found, the colony would be dead. Now, this equation applies to every resource: oxygen, amino acids, carbon compounds, nitrogen, various electronic components, and even worse, any catalysts, substances that are changed by the interaction of a process."

"The first critical point of scarcity," Richard interrupted, "defines the limits of growth or survival." He looked around with a self-satisfied smile, as Ian and the others turned to him.

"Well, it's an ecological point, and that's what these colonies are—closed ecologies. The first point of scarcity will define their possible limit, any bioscientist knows that. So you're saying that a number of these units had limited carrying capacity."

"At least a hundred are most likely dead by now," Ian continued, "unless they entered another star system for resupply and possible colonization. But from what Stasz has said of the survey, there were no signs of that."

"So far we've checked the fifteen nearest stars," Stasz responded.

"And nothing?" Shelley asked.

"Not a sign."

"It's damn peculiar," Shelley replied. "You'd have thought that the units would have naturally gravitated to the nearest star systems."

"Maybe none of them were appropriate," Richard interjected.

"Two of the systems had planetary bodies that might have been useful for resupply, but the others, except for the energy from the star, were next to useless," Stasz replied.

"Let's get back to the question of which direction to take," Ellen said, sensing that the rest of them would soon be off on a technical discussion that could last for days.

"Ah, yes," Ian responded, as if being drawn back from a drifting line of thought that he wished to pursue. "Which way . . ." His voice trailed off.

"How about thataway," Richard announced melodramatically, while pointing off vaguely toward the "down" direction of the room.

"Dr. Lacklin," Shelley said quietly, waiting for the laughter at Richard's comment to die down. "Dr. Lacklin, what about toward SETI Anomaly One and the galactic center?"

Ian brightened up at her suggestion.

"Precisely what I was leading to, of course," he said hurriedly. "You see, there was one general trend in the movement. *Colonial 237*, which was the second unit to depart, was headed straight for the galactic center, and our records show that one hundred thirty-five other units went within ten minutes of arc to either side of that point."

"Well, that narrows the volume tremendously."

"Still a bit of a problem, Ellen," Stasz replied.

Ellen groaned. "It only gives us an area about twenty-one thousand A.U. in diameter to search at a range of fifty light-years out."

Ian chuckled softly and gave Shelley a baleful glance. "I tried to explain this to the Chancellor, but do you think he cared about the mathematics of our search? Oh no. You see, a bright young graduate assistant had convinced a bunch of drone-head bureaucrats that this expedition could work." His normally high voice started to crack into falsetto. "Twenty-one thousand A.U." And shaking his head, he fell silent.

"Why the galactic center?" Richard asked.

"Why not? There were several stars they could orbit into along the path, and somehow it seemed appropriate. Sort of like going to the center of everything, if you will. And if we were to find anything in terms of life, I guess that would be the place to look for it. That, and the SETI contact back in 2018, coming straight out from the galactic center. Even though the contact point was estimated to be four thousand light-years away, it was still something to go for in all that immensity of space."

"Are there any other areas of such promise?" Stasz asked.

"No," Ian said softly, "the other colonies were pretty evenly distributed. A fair number going toward the thirty nearest stars, and, like I already said, the paradox of this is that in the first fifteen checked out so far, not one sighting has been made. If we head toward the galactic center, within a hundred light-years three stars not too far off the trajectory might be worth checking out. Twenty-three units used solar sails as their propulsion, and with our survey-ship telescopics, we can run a computerized scan as we head out. Forty of the units were using the old Orion concept—nuclear-blast pulsing."

"God, how primitive," Stasz muttered.

"Yeah, almost barbaric, but it worked. We might get lucky and detect a detonation or, at least, residual radiation from the pulsers. The ramjets will leave a certain amount of disturbance in their wake, and with luck, we can latch on. We'll have to trust to the nav-detection computer system to pick out anything and hope that there is some semblance of communication between them which we can home in on. Many of the units carried a powerful beacon system and we know the frequencies, so we can track on that, as well.

"So, unless one of my fellow travelers has another

suggestion, I guess we should point ourselves into the galactic core and hope."

"We do have fairly precise measurements on colonials *418* and *422*," Shelley interjected. "We could try for them first."

"I don't think it really matters," Ian replied despondently, "so what the hell, enter it into the log as we depart that we're locking onto the tracks of *418* and *422*. At least it will make us sound like we're doing something."

"You sound as if you don't expect to find any of those colonies," Ellen responded.

"By the Eye of the Crab," Stasz shouted, and he pointed to Richard and winked. Richard pulled a plastic pouch out of his pocket and tossed it to the pilot, who snatched it out of the air, pulled the straw out, and drained off so much of the contents that Richard's face fell even as Stasz's turned redder and redder.

"As I was about to say, nearly seventy-five percent of these Alpha-3 class survey ships never came back from their surveys. Hell, lady, chances are you'll die before we ever find one of Ian's bloody lost friends. Why the hell do you think the government gave this ship to your grant foundation? Two years ago they dumped a pretty penny into overhauling this crate and then the smart boys in Research and Development come up with a safer and faster design. Now if they scrapped this bucket some damn fool antispace senator would scream that we're wasting taxpayers' money. Of course nobody in DSSE wants assignment to this deathtrap, so some bright young fellow comes up with the idea of giving it to you damned stupid educators via the research foundation. Why, that's the perfect plan! This bucket sails off to oblivion, no one at DSSE is to blame, and in fact we get a bigger appropriation to build a replacement."

"So why are you along, my friend?" Richard asked.

"'Cause I had a little run-in with the Governor."

"Oh."

"Did you ever hear of his daughter?"

Richard Croce's and Ellen Redding's howls filled the room. Ian just turned scarlet. Only Shelley was strangely quiet.

"You're all crazy, you are," Stasz shouted. "I'll watch you laugh though when I punch us out of here in three hours. Is it the galactic center, then?"

Ian nodded his head sadly. Why not? Hell, it was as good as any area to search. They'd have to find at least one colony, that was plain. Maybe with a little luck they could score something in a year or so.

With a whispering hiss the *Discovery* slipped from its docking bay, the faint push from the back of the seat creating a sensation that "down" was at the rear of the command compartment. Ian looked across at Shelley, who was in the couch behind Stasz, and gave a reassuring smile. But she didn't need one. It was her first flight, and for her it was a moment full of wonder.

Ian listened in on the chatter over Stasz's comlink. He never figured out how a pilot could make sense of the nonstop commands as flight control sorted out the dozens of incoming and outbound flights.

"*Com Sat Rep 23A*, your approach to D-97 on 933 is open. Ah, *VCT 9-er*, you are cleared for entry into Restrict 9, approach at point-four M per. *Discovery 1* . . ."

"That's us," Stasz whispered.

"Out to depart line 8, cleared at your discretion. Good luck."

"*Discovery 1* up to point-one G on depart line 8," Stasz replied as his fingers danced across the green-lit board. The quiet *hiss*ing was suddenly punched out by a dull rumbling *throb* that pushed them back into their seats, then the booster flared to life as Stasz punched up an outside view astern on the main monitor so his passengers could watch departure.

The nexus point of the station was already a mile east-

ern, silhouetted by the backlighting of a half-phase Earth.
The skyhook beyond the nexus shone like a diamond, the
sharp, straightedged line descended toward Earth until it
finally disappeared from view. Jutting out from the cable
in all directions a host of spidery weblines curved away
into the infinity of space, a halo over 45,000 miles in
diameter, hanging above the Earth—the growing hub of
civilization's outward reach.

The passengers of *Discovery 1* were strangely quiet as
each one dealt with his inner fears. Stasz's taunting words
had a ring of truth to all of them. The odds were stacked
against the voyage, and all because a Chancellor wanted
to rid himself of some staff to open up positions for a
couple of new cronies.

"Take a good look at old mother Earth." Stasz laughed
softly. "You ain't gonna see no blue for a long time to
come. Jesus, it got so on my last trip out that I would
think more about blue skies and oceans than I even thought
about sex. Funny how the body misses some things more
than others out here."

"You're really not helping things," Richard replied.

"Not paid to help things." Stasz laughed. "Paid to fly
this crate and point out the realities to you folks. Hang
on, I'm bringing her up to three G."

He punched up the control buttons and the rumbling
roar increased in pitch as they were pushed deeper into
their seats. Ian rolled his head toward Shelley and saw
that she was absolutely enthralled with the whole thing.

She gave him an excited smile. "This is what it must
have been like for those first voyagers," she said, her
eyes alight with excitement. The only response she received were groans from Ellen and Richard.

Within minutes Richard noticed that the half planet of
Earth was noticeably receding, so that the entire planet
occupied less than half the screen. The Brasilia terminus
was still visible, looking more like a jewel in a spider's

web than a complex structure that housed half a thousand workers and docking ports for a hundred ships.

Stasz slowly throttled them up to 3.5 G and held the rate there for several long minutes. Ian knew it was simply a matter of showmanship on Stasz's part. They could just as easily have accelerated at 1 G as they cleared near-Earth space—and the ultimate effect would have been no different—but Stasz, like most pilots, wanted to "hot trail" it out and feel the pleasure of raw power under his control.

Let him have his fun, Ian thought. He was surprised to realize that he was enjoying himself. The historian in him was fantasizing, as well—just as Shelley was doing—imagining the feel of an old shuttle or HBV at lift-off. He settled into his couch and let the pulsing roar engulf him in a drowsy state. Suddenly the pressure intensified and he heard a muffled cry of dismay from Richard. Looking across to Stasz, Ian saw that the pilot had slammed the throttle to the wall. Stasz's eyes were wide and betrayed a maniacal gleam: he was getting off on the power.

They inched up past 4 and then started toward 4.5, and Stasz laughed with a high-pitched keen.

Great, the pilot was crazy!

The *Discovery* thundered away, slashing across space on its outward trajectory. And suddenly the rockets winked off.

A deep rolling sensation rose from Ian's stomach as they went from 4.5 to 0 in an instant. He had the unpleasant sensation that he was tumbling head over heels, and from her low, gasping groan he knew that Ellen Redding was already experiencing the worst of it. Stasz merely laughed.

"And into the universe!" he cried.

The disk of the Moon soon matched the Earth's in size, as Stasz called them to the forward cabin where they strapped themselves back into their cushioned couches.

"I've reviewed it with you once, but for one last time, here we go. We've cleared the major shipping lanes of near-Earth environment, and our nav system has come up clean, but to be on the safe side I've positioned our initial path five degrees of arc off the asteroid belt and will compensate once we've cleared that region. Remember, the translight jump will cause a momentary blackout and all of you will experience some degree of nausea, so have those damn bags ready. After the initial jump the ship's gravity inertia system will kick on, so remember that there will be one G aligned toward the long axis of the ship.

"Are you ready?"

They all nodded bleakly. Ian shot one final look at the small blue-green disk just barely visible on the video display. This great adventure was already starting to pale. Just what the hell was he doing there?

"Oh, by the way," Stasz shouted out with a laugh, "in one out of every ninety-seven point four jumps, the ship breaks up. We've never figured out why. Just thought you might like to know."

Ian looked at Ellen. She was tight-lipped but managed a cold grimace of a smile. He wasn't sure if it was a smile of genuine fear or one of resentment at the crazy scheme that had dragged her into space. Shelley, however, had a look of joyous anticipation. Richard was strangely quiet, and Ian suddenly realized that the doctor had narced himself out with a tranq shot.

"Here we go," Stasz shouted. "Crazy Stasz plays with light speed—and don't say I didn't warn you!" He pulled the lever that punched them into star drive.

Ian's vision blurred. He tried to focus on the disk of the Earth, but it was already lost to view. The sun shot into range of the camera focused astern, its once-yellow disk shifting through the lower end of the visual spectrum to infrared. The darkness of space around it distorted in a hazy shimmer. He could hear Stasz's high-pitched laughter and, as if triggered by it, experienced a swirling blackness of nightmarish dreams.

CHAPTER 4

THE SHIPBOARD ROUTINE WAS SOON ESTABLISHED. ELLEN avoided Ian and Richard and to their surprise soon fastened her attention onto Stasz, even though he was, in her own words, "merely a ship's driver, and not a very well-educated driver at that."

They were grateful for the respite. The vessel was small enough, as it was, but hidden in an aft storage compartment Ian soon found a quiet retreat where he could be alone with his thoughts. And it was there, several weeks after *Discovery*'s departure, that Richard came to him, bottle in hand.

"Ah, my good friend and fellow wizard," Richard intoned softly, holding up the precious bottle of gin for Ian's examination. "Come, my morose and melancholy colleague, life could be worse. You could be back at that damnable college with that thrice-damned Chancellor breathing down your neck. So come drain this precious liquid with me and rejoice that fortune has thus smiled upon us."

Ian smiled wanly and pushed aside a couple of crates to widen his little nook so Richard could crawl in.

Richard squirmed into the cubbyhole, uncorked the bottle, and offered it to him straight.

Ian screwed up his face and, with a quick tilt of the head, gulped down the scalding liquid. His eyes streamed rivers of tears; he coughed convulsively and struggled for breath, but soon the warming glow spread through his body.

Richard looked around the retreat and shook his head. He knew Ian to be a fairly typical intellectual neurotic, but the man was head of the project and their lives could depend on this neurotic's decisions. "Must say that you've got a nice little fortress here." He took the bottle from Ian, drained off a mouthful, and smacked his lips. "You certainly picked a nice place to hide out."

Ian gave Richard a twisted smile, already knowing what he was driving at. "You mean, retreat from reality."

"Now did I say that, my good man?"

"No, but we've known each other for twenty years. I can already tell you what you've been thinking about. Shall I?"

"By all means, second guess me."

"You're thinking that Ian Lacklin is a good enough sort of fellow to play a round of chess with, to talk a little historical bullshit with, to knock a drink down with on a rainy winter evening, but let's not push it beyond that.

"Yes, beyond that," Ian interjected, waving his arms, "beyond your typical foggy history teacher who spends most of his waking hours dreaming of a history he never could, or never will, interact with. Hell, man, a history teacher by his very nature avoids the reality of his own time by escaping into the past. Just think, Richard, just think for one minute, did you ever meet a history teacher who had both feet on the ground?"

"Well, I can think of—"

"Just a minute," Ian interrupted, "I mean a *real* history teacher, not some smashball coach disguised as a history teacher."

"Well, in that case, I guess..." His voice trailed off.

"Point proved! My colleagues and I are paid to examine that which can no longer be touched. History, the past. Oh, sure, we all dream at times of walking into that past and being one of the heroes. I know a skinny, gawky runt of a history prof who would give ten years off his life just to ride with Ghenghis Khan for one day. But really, if old Ghenghis ever showed up in his office, that guy would need a new set of underwear in ten seconds flat. That's my point: We're fine at examining a dead past, but to be part of the living present with its realities and dangers is another story."

"What are you driving at, Ian?"

"Look at us!" Ian shouted, and taking the bottle from Richard he popped off another gulp. "We've got a crazy as a pilot, a pimply grad-ass, and, God help us, old C.C. Then there's you. Pardon me, but you know your short-comings as well as I do. A doctor in the college clinic with a good grasp of pre-Holocaust medicine and a great grasp on the bottle. Finally there's me. Richard, we've been dumped, and you know and I know that if we ever get back, it will be a miracle. And I am not merely head of a project—I am in *command*!"

Good lord, he's right, Richard thought, trying to hold his expression straight. Ian Lacklin is in command of a ship, not some damned faculty subcommittee meeting, where the worst possible blunder that could be committed was that a room might get painted the wrong color, or another one of Ellen's damnable surveys would be forced upon a group of unwilling students.

"That scares you now, doesn't it?" Ian asked softly. "We are cruising out into totally unknown territory, in a vessel that is known to be unreliable, with a leader who is not fit to lead."

"So, what is the alternative?"

"You want the job?" Ian asked hopefully.

"Are you crazy? At least you're sober more than half the time." He paused.

"There's always Ellen..."

"She'd push both of us out the airlock at the first chance, if we ever gave command to her," Ian replied sadly.

"And after that 'crazy Stasz plays with star drive' routine, I think that issue is settled, as well," Richard responded. "So, friend, that leaves only you—a woolly-headed, slightly wimpish, and, in fact, altogether cowardly history professor as our fearless leader. Think of it, Ian, you might be famous someday—statues to our five-and-a-half-foot, overweight, bespectacled, receding hairlined..."

"Enough. You know, Richard, you're a great psychologist and a real help to someone's fragile ego."

"Oh, come on, Ian, you'll do all right. After all, if we don't come back, well, I guess that means we don't come back."

"Remarkably profound of you."

"Have another pull then, my friend, and let thine ego be restored."

For several long minutes the two friends sat in silence. Richard, not making the situation easy on Ian, kept him under a steady stare, trying to hold eye contact that Ian attempted to avoid. Finally the barrier broke down.

"There's one other thing," Ian whispered.

"I thought so." And there was no note of triumph in his voice, but rather a genuine sense of concern. Something had been gnawing at Ian from the moment of departure; maybe he'd finally get the answer.

"You know history is not the most popular of subjects back home," Ian said sadly. "What with this New Renaissance of High Tech that everyone is chasing, some of the early lessons have been forgotten. But ever since we launched, I've been thinking about a point that I daresay the folks back home never considered."

"And that is?"

"Montezuma and Cortez."

"I don't follow you."

"You know the story—Cortez and his six hundred kicked the Aztec Empire into oblivion."

"Yeah, I have some faint recollection of it."

"I've been thinking, you know, just letting my imagination run. Suppose Cortez had mixed it up with something different, something with, say, nukes—what would have happened to Spain then?"

"You've got me, Ian. Let's hear this theory of yours."

"I know these people, these people out of our past. I know them better than I know my neighbor, my students, or in some ways, even you, my friend. You see, Richard, I've devoted my life to studying those explorers and settlers out of the long-distant twenty-first century. I can speak Old English, Old Russian, and Old Japanese fluently, and I can get by in half a dozen others. I've read every single text and document that deals with the great Exodus. I feel more at home with the people of that period than I do in my own age. I can sense their wonder, their purpose, their passionate drive to settle space."

His voice drifted off for a moment, as if he was lost in thought, then suddenly he continued.

"Theirs was a grand epic, Richard, those first explorers, and now I'm afraid."

"Why?"

"Can't you see? To me it is a dream, a romance. Haven't you ever idealized a woman from afar? Think back to when you were young, Richard. Think of that heart-stopping moment, when the mere sight of her was enough."

Richard smiled vaguely and nodded.

"That is the life of a historian. An idealized romance from afar. And remember this, as well, Richard, remember when she was no longer idealized but came to your embrace. And then what finally happened?"

And Richard nodded sadly and understood.

"That is my first fear, my friend. The fear that an idealist has when reality finally confronts him. But the fears run deeper."

"As is to be expected from a typically neurotic type such as yourself. Hell, man, you wouldn't be happy if you only had one level of fear."

Ian shot him a look of reproach.

"Sorry. Go on then."

"As I said, I know these people better than I know my own contemporaries. I know the circumstances of why and how they left. Richard, with well over half a thousand units somewhere out there, has one of them ever come back?"

"Well, as I understand it, you just can't turn a million tons of mass around and 'come back,' as you say. At least I know that much about physics. The energy requirements alone—"

"Ah, but we're talking about ten centuries, my friend. Why didn't our exploratory teams to the nearest fifteen stars find some sign of them? By God, man, it's logical to assume that some of them would have checked out Centauri or Barnard's. Damn it, there's even a gas giant and iron-nickel asteroids around Barnard's. But we didn't find a single sign of them there. And for that matter, one of them could easily have looped around a star and returned. But not a sign, not a single damn sign."

"And you mention the exploratory teams that haven't come back."

"I've wondered on that, as well, and I'll place good money that our friend Stasz thinks about it."

"What are you driving at, then?"

"Suppose they found something that wouldn't let them come back?"

"Come on now, Ian, when I said you were neurotic I

was serious, but good heavens, man, don't make me diagnose you as a paranoid, as well."

"Interesting comment, Richard, 'good heavens.' What makes us associate the two?" Ian muttered as if musing to himself. "Must be medieval tradition and concepts. The heavens aren't good, Richard, they'll kill you in an instant. Just think, man, we've got this thin wall"—he tapped the side of the hull, which echoed hollow in the room. "That and an ethereal force field beyond are our only protection as we slip by at translight speed. Think if the nav system miscalculated and ran us up on a chunk of rock bigger than my fist, you wouldn't have 'good heavens' then."

"Stop trying to make me paranoid, too," Richard muttered. And with his eyes fixed on the hull behind Ian, he washed down another swallow of gin.

"But don't worry about it," Ian said with a soft smile, obviously pleased that he had caused a spark of fear in the usually unflappable Richard. "If it did happen there would be such a tremendous flash of energy that we would be vaporized before our synapses could register one screaming instant of fear."

"Aren't you comforting."

As if in response, a faint shudder ran through the vessel and Richard winced. Ian's heart skipped a beat, but he tried not to show it. The translight nav system worked after all, even while they were talking; sensing an approaching obstacle, it had shifted them around the mass, the inertia-damping system compensating for all but a fraction of the lateral forces.

"Shall we return to what you were saying?" Richard said softly.

"Ah, yes, my fears of the hostile universe. After all, if one is going to be afraid, why not make it a really big fear? Why not fear the whole universe? Tell me, good doctor, is there a word in your lexicon for an abnormal fear of the entire universe?"

Richard wasn't sure if Ian was joking or not, and he thought it best at this point not to find out.

"Do you mean a fear of alien life forms?"

"Perhaps. Remember, Doctor, we've only had faster-than-light travel for the last ten years. In fact, in this obsolete first-generation hulk, we will be venturing out farther than anyone from our century has dared, so far. Maybe we'll meet aliens, but I must confess that I doubt it. No, Richard, I'm sorry to say that I think we here at the far end of his neglected corner of the comos are truly alone."

"So what else is there?"

"Ourselves."

"You mean Ellen or Stasz or, heaven forbid, that assistant of yours. You think that kid is going to get seized by a transport of sexual frenzy and murder everyone else so that she can have you to herself." Richard chuckled slightly at the image of Ian's acned assistant suddenly unchained of her prim and proper nature, and as the image flowed, he realized that in fact it could be quite interesting.

"Come now, Richard. Shelley sees nothing in me. Our relationship is purely professional. I needed an assistant to manage my data during this trip, and since she wrote the damned grant, I figured she'd be the one to do it. But let's get serious now. When I said 'ourselves,' I meant it collectively."

"You mean those already out there."

"Precisely, Richard. We've set off on this voyage to find the Lost Colonies. 'Lost Colonies.' Lost by who's definition? They left us, didn't they? Have any of them come back?"

"No. At least, not that we know of."

"Then are they really lost? Damn it, man, it's not like some sixteenth-century sailor getting lost in the Pacific. The colonies left us of their own free will—they left us of their own free will, and maybe they don't want anything to do with us."

"I think that thought's a little foolish," Richard responded. "After nearly eleven centuries they most likely would be damn glad to get at least one letter from home."

"Maybe they would, but I'm fearful that some might not want us to drop in for a visit."

"Then if that's the case, we'll just thumb our noses, hook on the translight drive, and tell them to eat our cosmic dust."

"Don't be so superior about it. That's the biggest trap of all in this game."

"Come on, Ian, aren't you overreacting a bit? If they don't want to see us, that's fine with me. In fact, I really don't give a damn if I see them or not. No, let me rephrase that. I might want to find a colony if they have the right women. Didn't you say that one of the colonies was a women's consciousness group, and no men were allowed?"

"Yeah, *Colony 122*. It set off in this general direction. Reports indicate they had stored enough fertilized embryos and frozen sperm to keep them going for a hundred generations."

"What a paradise."

"I should drop you off on the all-male *Colony 123*."

"Maroon Ellen there. They wouldn't know what to do with her anyhow."

"Now, Richard!"

"It is a charming thought, though, isn't it?" Richard tried to stand up but merely succeeded in banging his head against a locker.

"Speaking of Ellen, that reminds me. She sent me off to look for you. She's planned one of her alleged gourmet meals and wanted your opinion on an arcane formula for something called brie."

"Popular late twentieth-century cheese. Quite big

among the alleged intelligentsia. I think I could help her out."

"Well, you better join her in the galley. She wants to serve up a genuine twentieth-century meal."

"God help us."

Richard turned and started to crawl out of Ian's hiding spot.

Suddenly Ian's hand was on his shoulder, restraining him. He looked back and saw the strain on Ian's face.

"What is it?"

"I haven't said it all," Ian whispered.

Richard settled back down.

"Go on then."

"Ellen's dinner points it out."

"How's that?"

"You, Shelley, the Chancellor, in fact, everyone envisions this voyage as a trip to find the Lost Colonies from eleven centuries ago. Look at Ellen: She's cooking up a dinner from the twentieth century as if she half expects that we'll dock with a colony and they'll come pouring aboard in polyester leisure suits, listening to Glenn Miller music, and ask us how our 'personal space' is."

Ian stopped for a moment and looked at Richard in exasperation. "Well, you're all wrong, all of you. It is the ancestors of the people that left eleven centuries ago that we are *now* looking for. They've had eleven hundred years to progress without the interruption of the Holocaust War. Good lord, Richard, that war took eight hundred years to recover from. Eight hundred years that we lived on the edge of extinction, and only in the last hundred years or so have we again equaled the accomplishments of the late twenty-first century. But those units that left us left intact—their memory banks laden with the sum total of man's knowledge to work on. It's estimated by some— Beaulieu, for example—that we've lost in excess of ninety-five percent of all records before 2087."

"So think of the opportunity," Richard said soothingly.

"Just think of it, man, you're the historian. You should be ready to kill for this chance—just to get aboard one of those ships and to be able to tap into its library. Damn it, Ian, just one ship's library would fill our computer memories to capacity, and still there wouldn't be enough. Return with that, my friend, and then see your books get published. Why, I didn't even think of that—*all* of us could get published and get on all the telepix interviews. We'd make a bundle, we would."

"Richard, just listen. You've heard of the Vikings, haven't you?"

"Barbarians from around the eighteenth century, right?"

"Close enough. Now just picture a Viking wandering into our society. How would we receive him?"

"Lock him up, most likely."

"My point is made."

"Come on, Ian, we're no barbarians."

"To them we might be. After all, they've got an eleven-hundred year jump on us if they progressed after their departure."

"If they've progressed. Remember, you yourself said they were closed ecosystems—chances are they're all dead. Anyway, I remember that there were quite a few on Earth that tried to adopt a steady-state system when the fear of shortages hit in the late-twentieth century. You yourself advanced the theory in your manuscript that in a small, closed ecosystem innovation and progress would probably be banned. So with that logic, chances are they've not gone much beyond our own capabilities."

Richard took another tug off the bottle and offered it to Ian. To be polite, he took another swig and then handed it back.

"So there, argument settled then."

"Yeah, I guess so," Ian replied reluctantly.

"You better get back to the galley. I bet Ellen is already at a rolling boil."

"Tell her I'll be along in a moment or two."

"All right."

Richard crawled out. And, standing up with a groan, he started for the door. Stopping, he turned and gave Ian a mischievous smile.

"Think we might find *Colony 122*? You know, the women's group."

"I don't think so, but if we do, what makes you think they'll take you?"

"Hell, Ian, remember I used to be M.D. at the Auraria Normal College for Women, in the Dakota Territories."

"And you barely made it across the border before you were arrested for malpractice and morals charges."

"Ah, now, Ian, you know my uncle the regent of medicine was able to prove the lie those humorless people had perpetrated against me." With a laugh he closed the door behind him.

Colony 122, Ian thought. That would be one of the easy ones. It was the *500* series that he had not discussed with Richard. The last ones up, built in the 70s and 80s. The exiles. A fair percentage of them had headed in toward the galactic center along with the more innocuous *1–400* series. What really scared him was the exile units and the 500 series. They might be ticking bombs. They were the disenfranchised, the dispossessed of a world tottering toward war—the refugee colonies and the colonies made up of entire ethnic and political groups exiled away from Earth. The 500 series with its liberation groups: the Kurd nationalists, the Botswanian Liberation Group, Dr. Franklin Smith's political penal unit, or L-3 519, and the Pan-Zionist Russian Nationalists. It was groups like that which gave Ian the real fear that he could not express to his comrades.

Such groups seemed slightly romantic now. They were romantic because 1100 years separated them from the present. And as long as they were so distant, they were safe and fascinating to an age now safely run by the Democratic Bureaucracy, wherein nothing could overcome the inertia of the worldwide state. But he could come face to face with the direct descendants of groups that might not feel too friendly about Earth, and the thought gave him the chills.

He stood up, stretched, and turning, looked down at the small suitcase-size crate that he had been sitting on. Stasz had pointed it out to him while doing an inventory.

Ian had been sitting on a thermomine, a nuclear device capable of vaporizing a quarter-mile asteroid or a million-ton colony in a flash. The *Discovery* had carried hundreds of such mines when it briefly served on a navigation-clearing detail just before being turned over to the grant foundation. This one mine had not been removed, either through an oversight, or because the logistics officer didn't want to go through the paperwork necessary to remove a thermo device and transport it down to Earth.

Ian gazed at the crate, his curiosity aroused. Finally it got the better of him and he unsnapped the fasteners that held the box shut then peeked inside. It was a little disappointing somehow; he had expected warning signs and sirens to flash on and the mine to look like some incarnation of evil.

It was simply an ugly black ball with half a dozen silver projections locked upright. An instruction manual was hooked to one of the projections; picking the booklet up, he flipped it open.

Notice from the Manufacturer—Clearance Assured Inc.

Congratulations on selection of the enhanced AB-23A adjustable-blast clearance apparatus. Satisfaction assured when operated properly. Any and all complaints looked into at once by our experienced quality control personnel.

Be sure to read this operations manual and attached errata sheet before attempting use.

Ian skimmed through the booklet and found the errata sheet. It was printed in bright red ink. He examined it closely.

Warning!!! Warning!!! Warning!!! Starting with the 23A series, arming achieved by pushing down all six levers which will trigger warning devices. In response to complaints that dropping the device in gravity conditions might cause it to detonate, an additional triggering is now required. To activate FINAL COUNT DOWN: *pull up*, repeat, *pull up* last lever. Unless otherwise programmed, detonation will then occur in ninety seconds. Nonradio detonation has been chosen to prevent arming by high solar activity or broadcast from transmitters in nearby spacecraft. Check your manual for timer settings. Default detonation interval is 90 seconds. This safety feature is added at the request of former dissatisfied users, their heirs, and assigns and has been implemented for your convenience.

Ian stuffed the sheet into the middle of the book. Then, closing the case to the mine, he stuck the booklet into his back pocket.

The object should have filled him with blind terror, but for some reason Ian felt a certain sense of quiet resolution. The Montezuma and Cortez argument was never far from his mind these days. He was a historian and knew the possibilities.

So he had asked Stasz not to tell the others about the device. Cortez had burned his ships to prevent his men from escaping from the expedition. Ian tried to push the thought aside that he might have to burn his ship, as well, before the expedition ended.

It was no surprise to Ian that Ellen's dinner was excellent. She had even produced the right wine for the occasion, and after the first bottle of Brinar Chablis '64, Richard had, for the moment at least, settled into a polite conversation with their hostess for the evening.

"But, Ellen, I thought you objected to spirits. Eight weeks ago you wanted to dump my treasured emergency rations overboard."

"You mean that I wanted to lighten our vessel of a noxious brew one step removed from rat poison." Ellen smiled for a moment, her freckled face lighting up with a malevolent glow. "Of course, it was a mistake, my dear Richard."

"I'm glad to hear you say that. And I must in return compliment you for this amazing repast."

"I am thankful for your appreciation, Richard, and I was going to say my earlier move was a mistake. You see, I think keeping that rat poison was just perfect, considering who I hope it will eliminate."

"Charmed, Ellen, simply charmed," Richard muttered as he produced a cigar and prepared to ignite it. Ian feared an explosion on her part and he knew Richard was simply baiting her. He could see her seething under the red-faced smile but she didn't let go, and there was an almost audible sigh of relief around the table.

Of course, he could half guess the reason—she would occasionally smile in Stasz's direction. So, the cabin fever was already setting in, and her original disdain for the "ship's driver" was starting to thin. Stasz was attempting to ignore her, but that was difficult with only five people in the room. As the light conversation flowed back and forth, Ian was fascinated by the subtle interplay between the two of them as Ellen tried not to appear obvious, Stasz tried to ignore her while making yet another pass at Shelley, and Richard laid out bait and traps for both of them to fall into.

Well, this craft is turning in a regular little potboiler, Ian thought as he settled back into his chair, bumming one of Richard's precious cigars.

He was lost in thought for several minutes until Shelley's voice brought him back into the conversation's flow.

"I said, don't you agree, Doctor?"

"Agree, ahhh, I'll have to think—"

"You weren't listening again." There was a soft chastisement in her voice, like a mother gently scolding a favorite child. "I was saying that I think the Chancellor is most likely the head of the Provincial Department of Educational Services by now."

They fell silent for a moment.

"Yeah, his glory, our lives," Richard muttered.

"It might be a little more complex than that," Shelley responded. "After all, he had a number of reasons for putting you three out here. You were all known to be an opposition to him in the faculty, and as part of the promotion process, you people would be able to evaluate him. I think, however, that there might be more to it than that."

Suddenly their conversation was drowned out by the electronic wail of the ship's alarm. Ian could feel his heart flutter on the edge of a palpitation. Ellen assumed her classic "oh, my, I'm so flustered" pose. Richard attempted to gently pull on his cigar and exhale with a display of panache, but the sudden tremble of his hand gave it away. Only Shelley and Stasz broke the tableau and, pushing away from the table, they ran forward to the control center. The ship suddenly lurched and there was a momentary sensation of falling away as the vessel performed a radical shift in its course and the dampening system overloaded in an attempt to compensate.

"Debris or asteroid," Richard muttered.

"Holy shit!" It was Stasz's voice echoing down the corridor.

"Dr. Lacklin, come quickly!" Shelley cried.

Ian got up from the table and, with a show of bravado, he looked at Ellen and smiled.

"Would you mind clearing the dishes, Ellen, while I attend to the problem up forward."

"Shove the damn dishes," Ellen snapped, "let our fat medico scrub them." Pushing Ian aside, she started forward, with Ian at her heels.

Entering the forward cabin, they climbed to the command and control center, where Stasz was already strapped into his couch with Shelley in the nav-com position beside him. The vessel lurched again, nearly knocking Ian off his feet. Climbing up the ladder, he finally came up alongside of Ellen, who was peering over Stasz's shoulder at a display board that was all but incomprehensible to him.

"How bad is it?" Ian whispered.

"Bad? It's fantastic," Shelley exulted. "We might have something."

"What!"

"Hang on a minute, Doc," Stasz muttered as his fingers raced across the control panel. Hooking on his mike, he watched the display for a moment then started calling up more data.

"Confirm, configuration, ship relative 21.34.45.01 hours R.A., 00,02 Dec."

Within seconds the data design snapped across the largest of the monitors on the display board.

"Jesus, it's a thousand K across," Stasz murmured. "I think we've definitely got something here."

"What is?" Ellen asked.

"That's why the alarm went off. I programmed ship's nav to sound an alarm and automatically home onto any largely metallic object we encountered. Well, here we are."

Stasz looked over his shoulder and smiled at Ian.

"You're in luck, Doc, I think we've just found your first colony."

"But a thousand K across? They never built anything that big," Ian muttered.

"Yes they did," Shelley said meekly, fearful at correcting her mentor. "Solar sails."

"But out here, why keep them deployed? The solar wind is negligible. There isn't any evidence of a laser drive base behind them."

"We'll soon find out why," Stasz interjected. "Our ship has already locked on and is three days out with only a mild deviation from our original course."

He scanned the display board again, called for a reconfirm, then looked back at Ian with a puzzled expression.

"Curious."

"What's that?"

"They're heading inbound toward Earth at point zero one two L.S. I thought you said all these guys were trying to get away. This one is hanging sails to the wind where there is no wind and running inbound."

Ian looked at the display showing him that soon he would come face to face with a world out of the past.

He felt the cold stir of fear.

CHAPTER 5

Colonial Unit 181
First Completion Date: 2031
Primary Function: Standard Japanese Colonial/Manufacturing Unit
Evacuation Date: Estimated June 2083, one of the first units recorded to have completed its conversion and departure.
Overall Design: Standard Mitsubishi Design Unit Double Torus. Maximum Population Potential (MPP) of 37,500 with standard mix of software/hardware industry and experimental design work on self-replicating processing system.
Propulsion: Solar Sail with matter/antimatter boost.
Course: Galactic Core.
Political/Social Orientation: Hierarchical Corporate Model with head of each family responding to subsystem leader. Standard Social Orientation and Interactive Systems.

"Program engage, jump-down to match V-1, target Alpha, close to point zero zero one A.U., engage."

Stasz turned in his couch and smiled at the rest of the crew. "Be sure you're strapped in," he said with a laugh. Reaching into his pocket, he pulled out the half-chewed stub of an unlit cigar and waved it at Shelley.

"You sure that belt is strapped tight? I don't want you falling out of your couch, the way you did last time." He reached over as if to help her, but she hurriedly showed him that it was snugged in tight around her hips and the cross belting of the shoulder harness was properly secured.

A high-pitched warning Klaxon sounded—the thirty-second mark to jump down.

"Don't worry, folks, this one ain't so dangerous. Only a point twenty-four percent probability of disintegration."

"How reassuring," Ellen whispered.

It was their second jump of the day, the last one having been completed only minutes earlier. They had closed in on their target and jumped down to a relative speed of zero in relation to their original trajectory. But since the target was in fact inbound toward Earth, they were taking a short jump to close to maneuvering range.

"Ten seconds and sequencing start."

Ian could feel the inertia-dampening system hum to life, and it was almost a signal for his stomach to get ready with its usual reaction.

The jump-down hit. Overall velocity was still sublight so the effects weren't too bad, but it still took Shelley several minutes to help Ian with his post-jump cleanup.

Ian could hear the soft gasps of astonishment from Richard and Ellen, and looking past his own tragic problems, he saw a sight that was stunning, after weeks of Doppler-shifted light.

Even from thousands of K out, the sails of the vessel filled a good part of their visual range.

"Look, Ian, I think it's a double torus," Shelley said.

Ian realized that for the first time she wasn't calling him Dr. Lacklin.

Ian looked to Stasz's radar display and Shelley's keen vision was confirmed by the screen. A standard double torus. Not the most efficient design, but fairly popular nevertheless.

"Do you have any idea which one it is?" Ellen asked.

"Too early to tell. Shelley, could you access my ship configuration data file? Cross-check it with known double torus designs that headed out on this trajectory."

She started working while the others fell into silence as the vessel and its sails filled an ever-larger portion of their field of view. Stasz had programmed their jump to perfection, with just enough residual velocity so they could safely close in.

Ian suddenly realized he was trembling. He wasn't sure if it was from fear, anticipation, or, most likely, a healthy mixture of both.

"I know how you feel, my dear friend," Richard said, patting him on the shoulder. "The first night of my marriage to Ethel, I was trembling just like you."

"And she was most likely trembling with disgust until she finally got that divorce," Ellen whispered *sotto voce*.

It broke the tension enough that all of them could laugh for a minute.

As they watched, the double ring came closer into view, so that its central support shaft could soon be made out in the faint glow of deep space starlight.

"Have you set the radio for the frequencies I suggested?" Ian asked.

"The signal will pulse out on all frequencies you mentioned, along with several I think might be worth looking into."

Ian activated his headset and nodded for Stasz to open the line.

He looked around at his colleagues and tried to conjure up the correct words in Old English.

"This is Earth vessel *Discovery* calling, Earth vessel *Discovery*. Please respond."

Nothing.

"Asleep at the switchboard most likely," Stasz said in a reassuring voice. "Hell, there can be times when no one is on the com for hours. I daresay they don't expect a visitor to drop in every day, the way we do."

"This is Earth research vessel *Discovery* approaching and requesting docking information."

"Ah, Dr. Lacklin, try Japanese," Shelley said.

"How's that?"

"According to your data, there were twenty-three double torus designs, of which eight used sails. And of those eight, six were Japanese."

He tried to remember his Old Japanese, and after a minute or so, he believed he got off a reasonable message. Still no response, so Stasz looped recording of Ian's request while they settled back.

"These ships have automatic piloting systems that detect and give alarm for any object bigger than a pea that approaches within ten thousand K," Ian said softly. "It could be that no one has gotten into the control room yet. If anyone's alive in there."

"There's significant damage to the sail area," Stasz interjected. "Number of lines parted, numerous punctures, I detect holes larger than one K in the central area. And I think we're picking up a reading here that indicates a significant holing on the main shaft of the vessel."

"We'll soon know," Ian muttered as they continued to close in.

Ian had read about them for years and had watched them on countless videos, but nothing, absolutely nothing had prepared him for the sheer awesome size of a colonial unit. It filled the entire sky, as if it would somehow encompass the universe. Nothing in his experience could possibly compare with the massive double-curve sweep of the twin torus that slowly wheeled on either side of them as they closed in toward the docking ring on the main shaft.

The sheer mass of the object was enough to create a minor gravitational disturbance that required Stasz to provide a slightly increased deceleration as they closed in.

As the four of them floated toward the docking bay, Shelley passed out hard copies of the ship's design and schematics of the blueprints now that the particular designation of the ship had been confirmed by exterior markings. They had already detected half a dozen unrepaired holes in the vessel, one of them a twenty-meter puncture through the main shaft. So there was little if any hope of finding any life.

Ian was dreading the encounter for fear of what he would find. In the three hours of closing there had been no signal of any kind. There was no sign of interior lighting and no heat dissipation from the coolant radiators.

Sealing himself into his bulky pressure suit, Ian settled into the docking bay and waited, listening intently as Stasz called out the ever-closing range.

There was a faint jar as the adjustable docking unit connected with the hull of the other ship. The green light over the docking-bay hatch turned yellow, and he could feel the pressure suit crinkling as the docking chamber depressurized.

The light overhead changed to red. Ian looked at the other three and nodded. There they were, four heroes, ready to go forward in the name of Democratic Bureaucracy. Four heroes, and he couldn't help but laugh, his high-pitched giggle sounding somewhat foolish and slightly hysterical.

He punched the button in front of him and the hatch slid open. They were locked up against the side of the colony, pressed against a nonrotating collar in the middle of the central shaft. A manual docking door was in front of him, instructions in Japanese, English, and Russian written across it.

Within seconds he had deciphered their meaning, and, grabbing the two handles alongside the door, Ian attempted to rotate them.

He spun in the opposite direction.

After several minutes of cursing and sweating, the other three helped brace him into position and he tried again.

As if on rusted hinges, the handles gave way slowly then suddenly they broke free and started to spin of their own volition. The doorway slid open. A slight puff of air came out of the ship. Ian looked up and his mind blanked out in horror as the ship's radio overloaded with his hysterical screams.

Ellen was back in the corner, still clawing at the escape latch back into their own ship, which would not open with the outside door unlatched. Yes, he could see that now. Panicked, Ian looked around, the only sound his own convulsive breathing and Ellen's soft whimpers coming over the radio set.

"Ian, it's all right, it's all right." It was a soft, soothing voice. Richard, yes, it was Richard.

He could feel the hands on his shoulder. His friend's face was barely visible behind the helmet, and his own vision was obscured by the moisture from his hyperventilation.

He looked back and started to turn his head.

"No, not yet, Ian. Don't look back until you're ready."

"What—" He started to sob again. "What—Richard, what is it?"

"It's a body, Ian," Richard said softly, "it's nothing but a body mummified by the low pressure and dry air. It can't hurt you now, Ian. He just gave you a start when the change in pressure made him drift out of the airlock toward you."

"Yeah, just a start." Ian could feel his self-possession on the edge of falling apart again.

"Take a few more deep breaths and when you feel ready you can turn around."

"Where is he?"

"Shelley moved him back into the colony's airlock. She's waiting for us in there. I'm going over to Ellen now." He let go of Ian, and, pushing off from the wall, he floated over to where Ellen hung like a cat clinging to a sheer wall. Her sobbing still filled the headset.

Ian took a couple of more deep breaths and slowly turned.

As she poked around the interior of the colony's airlock, Shelley was barely visible except for her headlamp. While she searched around, she absently hung on to the mummified body with one hand.

Bracing himself, Ian pushed forward into the ship.

"Dr. Lacklin, I've found the airlock into the main corridor of the central shaft.

"Wait a minute, we better close the hatch behind us before continuing on in."

Ian looked back toward Richard and Ellen.

"Go on without us," Richard said. "I'm taking Ellen back in and giving her a stress pill."

Stress pill! Hell, he was the one the damn mummy banged into. Out of the corner of his eye he examined the body that Shelley was still hanging on to. A cold grimace of desiccated flesh and bone stared back at him out of lifeless, haunting sockets. He looked away.

Shelley, ignoring his fear, floated back to the docking door and closed it. Looking around the room, she noticed some Velcro stripping along one wall and without any ceremony pushed the mummy up against it. The fastabs on the body's uniform locked him into place. Leaving him on the wall, she floated back to Ian.

As she passed by him there was a flash of a smile that made Ian shudder. She was enjoying this!

"Want me to open this one?" she asked.

He nodded and closed his eyes. Would he ever be able to open a door again?

She turned the handle. There was a faint whisper of air as the pressure equalized. Something bumped against him. He wanted to scream, but with a supreme effort he repressed it. Opening his eyes, he discovered that Shelley was up against him.

He half suspected that she had banged into him on purpose, and a slightly mischievous smile almost confirmed it. There were no bodies inside, however, and together they pushed into the main corridor and started to explore.

"Shelley, Ian, this is Stasz. You better prepare for your return. Your in-suit reserve is below twenty percent."

Ian checked the elapsed time on his arm-mounted watch. Nearly six hours and not one percent of the vessel explored. They hadn't even gotten out of the main shaft area.

The sheer number of bodies overloaded his senses, but he had slowly grown inured to their presence or he was simply in shock and the reaction would hit later.

The forms of death were varied and frightening. Everywhere the dead leered at them, some gently floating by as the opening of long-locked blast doors and passageways triggered gentle currents in air that had not moved for centuries. Most of the cabins still held some air, but neither Shelley nor Ian dared to remove their helmets to try it. The command and control enter had been totally destroyed by a hulling—the impact that had punched a twenty-meter hole clear through the vessel with an egress puncture nearly fifty meters across.

Most of what they explored were various access passageways, docking terminals, and the guidance center for the ship's sails, where half a dozen desiccated forms were still strapped to their couches.

"Dr. Lacklin, I'm in what appears to be a communications center on level three, section four. Would you please join me?"

Turning about, he floated back up the corridor that she had followed only moments before. He pushed past a small body that held an even smaller form to its breast— he didn't look closer.

There was a faint light coming out of a room. He pushed his way in and to his surprise found that she had managed to locate a backup lighting system that could still function. A soft, diffused light radiated from overhead panels.

Shelley noticed his look of surprise. "Apparently the power grid hooking into this area is still intact and there are some backup batteries."

The room was circular with a number of windows on one side that looked out over the docking bay. As Ian went up to the window, he could see the *Discovery* docked on the next level down, or at least in the direction that his feet were pointing.

"It looks as if they stayed alive in here for some time after whatever it was hit them." She pointed to a number of boxes and empty emergency food containers that floated in the room along with the four bodies.

"Poor bastards. Damn it, Shelley, there must have been close to forty thousand living here. I'd have thought that damage control could have brought this ship on line again."

"I've been thinking about that, Dr. Lacklin. Look at the damage. Primary ship functioning area totally destroyed. Power reactor destroyed, main communications, data storage banks, and transport lines to the two wheels, damaged or destroyed. Eight major hull hits, all to vital areas. Two or three at the same time they could have bypassed and still managed to restore service. But not eight at once. Taking out those eight at the same time was fatal, and the occupants stayed trapped in each of their emergency chambers till the oxygen ran out. It's possible some might have lasted for weeks. What a horrible death..." Her voice trailed off.

"You think there's any chance of calling up ship's records?"

"Just a moment, Doc."

Shelley floated to the far corner of the room and hovered next to a body. For several minutes she twisted the body back and forth and suddenly the hand snapped off the body. He could hear a faint cry of dismay and felt at least a little pleasure at the realization that even Shelley was affected by this charnel house.

"Dr. Lacklin, how good are you at deciphering Old Japanese?"

"Not too good. I can speak it, but that's about it."

"Damn, this body had a notebook clutched to it. It might be worth looking at."

"I have the dictionaries back aboard ship."

"Speaking of back aboard ship," Stasz interrupted again, "listen, Doc, I have no desire to board that graveyard in search of your bodies. You're down to seventeen percent of reserve so would you kindly get your butts back where they belong. Shelley, at least get your butt back, I like it better than our rotund professor's gludius maximus, or whatever it is that Croce calls it."

Shelley started for the door still holding the notebook with the clawlike hand clinging to one side. Ian turned away for a moment and looked back out the port. His view was framed by the two wheels, above and below him, spinning slowly against the backdrop of an endless sea of stars. All the key points of the vessel struck, probably simultaneously—dooming all aboard. He looked out across the stars and shivered.

"I figured I should share this with all of you. I must confess that it changes the complexion of this mission"— Ian hesitated for a moment—"perhaps to the point of abandonment."

He looked around the room at his companions. Coming from a desk-bound civilization where meetings were the form of business, and the form required desks and chairs, the concept of a meeting in zero G had a slightly ridiculous quality. There were no desks to define territory and no seating with the leader at the head. Rather they floated around a room and copies of paperwork were tossed back and forth after being attached to clipboards. Stasz wasn't helping matters any by floating upside down relative to the rest of them.

Ian tried to gauge their reactions. The meeting was more a ritual; they already knew the information to be discussed and a general feeling had already been arrived at. But he wanted to be sure.

"Look, Ian," Ellen said quietly, "this happened nearly three hundred years ago. Three hundred years ago our Democratic Bureaucracy was at war with the Chin. Today the Chin are our closest allies."

"Let me go over it one more time, Ellen. And anyhow, I think you as a collective psychologist should know the theories of Constant Social Lines in relationship to an isolated society."

"It's a theory and I'm out here to prove it or disprove it, that's why I think this is absurd."

"Let's hear him out, Ellen, then you can attack him."

Ellen glared at Richard, who returned her stare with a mock bow that sent him tumbling head over heels until Shelley helped to stabilize him.

"Here we go then," Ian stated as formally as he could, but his voice was pitched too high and the nervousness showed.

"I've worked five days straight on the translations. In the interim Stasz and Richard managed to explore part of one torus and I think we can confirm that absolutely no one is left alive in there." He gestured vaguely toward the window where silhouetted on either side were the twin wheels rotating on their endless journey.

"This unit departed Earth in the year 2083 and is referred to as *Unit 181*. I've provided you with all my notes concerning its history. We've retrieved some Holo core memories but I don't have the equipment to use them.

"Several more notebooks have been recovered and I plan to analyze them, but I think the first one is good enough to go on."

He looked down at the notepad strapped to his knee.

"Most of the notes in the book were poetry. Rather nice stuff, called haiku. Our long-dead friend Miko was a sensitive individual. A longer poem on page twenty-three of the notebook gives us an interesting clue. He describes the blue sun of his childhood, which he now misses. Stasz and I have checked it out and this vessel could have come out of Delta Sag. Which means these people made it to a star eighty-two light-years from Earth and, as near as I can estimate, spent only twenty-odd years in orbit about that star and then began the long journey back to Earth. There are in fact four references to this sun. The next to the last poem is not a haiku, but more in the tradition of the nineteenth-century Romantics. In that poem the writer speaks of the mission they have set.

> To warn our forefathers in halls undreamed,
> And seek again the light that was,
> As we speak to the gods of the sleeping giant,
> Revenge of their sons, long dreamed dead.

Ian looked around the room again. The rest were silent. He had a brief mental flash of the vacant staring faces that had populated his classroom. But these people were listening to him, and he felt a surge of satisfaction.

"The last statement is a diary-type entry that makes one thing very plain—they were attacked. I'll read the last entry."

He knew this was rather pedantic, but he couldn't help but play on the dramatic; after all, he was a historian.

"'It is seventy-four hours since the Alpha/Omega strike. I look out at our twin wheel, our home, our world. The lights are still on in the Ag section, batteries...' The next line is illegible and then picks up again. 'My eyes see, but they cannot make me believe. My entire world is dying, it is dying and they have murdered us. Murdered us. It is the end and there is nothing. Our crypt shall journey across the sea of eternity, a voyager of quiet death. And so I join the others as the lights of my world fade away forever...'"

Ian felt a strange turmoil within. The young poet had written this to him, far more sure of the immortality of his verse than any Earthly poet. For in space the script would last, like its poet, for eternity.

"I've backplotted the heading," Stasz interjected, breaking the melancholy silence. "If acceleration ceased at current speed they would have left Delta Sag three hundred and ninety-seven years ago."

"How far to Delta Sag, Stasz?" Ellen asked.

"Two months."

Ellen looked at Ian with a challenging smile.

Ian hesitated, trying to buy time. "We've got to be logical about this one. First there is a wealth of information aboard this ship. This could keep an archaeological team busy for the next century. It's the first time anyone from our modern age has stepped aboard a vessel from the twenty-first century."

"Come on, Ian, stop being such a historian and start thinking like an explorer," Ellen replied. "I'm not interested in dead things, I want living people to sample. One of those things"—and she shuddered,—"in there might interest you as you cut 'em up to see what they had for breakfast, but that information is useless in my book. They came from this Delta Sag, I want to go there and find out more."

"There's the next point to consider, as well. This colony was murdered. Someone or something out there killed them. They could kill us!"

Now his emotions were taking hold.

They hesitated for a moment on that one and Ian pressed in. "I think we should stay here, study this one in further detail, and knowing there is something hostile out here, we have every legitimate excuse to return back home, report our findings, and then get back to our lives."

"From what I've heard of your Chancellor," Stasz interjected, "I don't think the sight of you four would be very welcome."

"To hell with the welcome," Ian replied. "What can he do to us? We found a colony and that's that."

"A dead one, Ian," Richard said. "I think our dear Chancellor is more interested in living proof than a floating morgue. Remember his famous comment at last year's board meeting: 'I am not an intellectual, I am an administrator.' That administrator will not be pleased with a dead *Colonial Unit 181.* He'll want live finds, finds that occur after the three years mandated by his office. Anyhow, my curiosity is aroused. Hell, we've come this far, why not finish it and go on to Delta Sag?"

"I'm curious, too," Stasz said.

Ian knew they were beating him; he had expected that from the beginning. For some strange reason their curiosity had been whetted. The fear of this attacker now acted like a candle drawing the moth in.

He looked at Shelley, but her only response was a shrug and a smile. Finally she leaned over and whispered.

"Come on, Ian, stop acting like a historian. The people aboard that ship are dead. Think of the chance of meeting some that are alive."

Ian looked back out at the turning wheel. A rumble ran through the *Discovery* and suddenly there was a faint return of gravity as Stasz piloted them up between the twin toruses. A flickering glow shone through the communications bay of *Colonial Unit 181*, and in the cold light he could make out the bodies floating on their eternal voyage.

At least that fear was gone. He had felt himself encased within a haunted fragment of the universe, as the souls of the dead still traveled on a journey that in another seven hundred years would bring them within sight of their ancestoral home.

He knew, as well, that even though they were departing, the ghosts would stay with his soul. The ghosts would come to haunt him in his nightmares of bodies floating in out of the darkness.

Stasz rotated the *Discovery*, and the nav computers took over. Soon they were pointed straight in at a steady blue light. Ian closed his eyes and braced for the jump that would take them to Delta Sag and the answer that all but he wanted.

CHAPTER 6

Colonial Unit: 27

First Completion date: 2031

Primary Function: Friends of the Light Colony. Anglo-American Peace Activist Group. In response to the growing concern over the second Kwajlein incident, this was the first of the "peace experiment" units that led the way for over one hundred utopian concept colonies.

Evacuation Date: According to Copernicus Base Record, June 6, 2086; however, Mars Base Hatley claims unit left nearly nine months later. Beaulieu believes Mars Base confused this with the "Second Friends of the Light Colony."

Overall Design: Standard Cylinder, first generation, 1200 meters by 300 meters.

Propulsion: Standard Modification Design, strap-on ion packs mounted to nonrotational central shaft.

Course: Galactic Core.

Political/Social Orientation: *Unit 27* was the first of the "Utopian" experiments modeled after the early-nineteenth-century Utopian movement; as such was the leading model of what would become a significant percentage of the twenty-first-century colonies. This unit attempted to model its government after consensus, with the guiding principle that a total concensus would be needed for any action. Therefore, a single dissenter could resist or stop an entire process. Second, violence of any kind was abhorred. Third, silent meditation was often the path to understanding.

The detection alarm did not cause the same thrill of fright that the first one had created, but the fact that it awoke him from a deep sleep caused Ian to flop around in confusion for several minutes until his glasses were in place and he was dressed sufficiently to appear in public.

The rest of the crew was already gathered around Stasz, with Ellen hanging very close to his shoulder. She had thrown on a light nightgown that clung tightly to her more than ample frame. Richard had already noticed that she was pressing her breasts into Stasz's arm and he gave Ian a sly nudge. Of course, they both knew what was coming, and settled back, anticipating her explosion with as much pleasure as they did the data racing across the monitors and spewing from the hard-copy displays.

As usual Shelley was in the seat next to Stasz, and she started interpreting the data while Stasz busied himself with ship commands.

"It's on a near-parallel course," Shelley muttered. "Relative ship trajectory R.A. twenty-one hours, forty-three minutes; declination five degrees north, range estimate one light-year, more or less."

"Good lord, Stasz," Richard exclaimed in surprise, "how the hell could we detect that?"

"Their automatic beacon," Ian replied. "The last one was out because the beacon had been hit in the strike.

This one is still functioning. It's nothing more than a signal burst and our ship's computer picked it up."

"Ahh, Dr. Lacklin, my printout reads that this thing is definitely Earth origin. Shall we go for it?"

"What the hell, that's what we're here for, Stasz." Ian shrugged and started to walk away.

Just before he closed the cabin door a loud smack echoed through the room. With a start Ian looked back, as Stasz staggered away from Ellen.

"How dare you?" Ellen shrieked, her features flushing scarlet.

"Listen, lady," Stasz intoned with mock seriousness, "where I come from a woman who presses up against a man who has been deep spaced for three months is obviously asking for some support. So I figured my free hand could provide that support."

Ian held the door open as Ellen glided out of the room in a royal huff. The moment Richard caught his eye they both broke out into rolling peals of laughter. Ian decided it was time for the cracking of another bottle.

"This looks like two in a row," Ellen said, her comment reflecting the dread they all felt as they surveyed what most likely was a dead colony.

The unit was less than a thousand meters away, turning slowly, outlined in sharp relief by the starlight and *Discovery*'s spotlights.

"I'm picking up a hot reactor," Stasz said hopefully. "Trace emissions. Their power supply is still good."

Stasz jockeyed them around the cylinder for a closer examination. There was no direct view into the unit since the colony was coated with heavy shielding in order to cut down the radiation exposure for the inhabitants. External light was admitted to the colony by a complex series of mirrors, and Stasz maneuvered toward one with the hope of getting a reflected view of the inside.

"There, in that mirror!" Shelley cried. "Look at the one to the right of the main antenna, do you see it?"

"If we're seeing light," Ian replied, "at least we know their power grid is still up."

In a vain attempt to appear calm, Ian had started a third read through of the *Thermomine Manual*. But the possibility of life aboard the ship was too much for him. Returning the manual to his back pocket, he started to pore through the hardcopy charts, quickly looking back at the cylinder for reference.

"The docking ports are on either end of the cylinder, Stasz. Shall we move in?"

Stasz started to maneuver in for final approach.

"Who's going?" Ian asked quietly.

Shelley turned expectantly and he gave her the nod. He looked at Ellen, half expecting her to back away after the last experience, but to his surprise she mumbled a brief reply about earning her keep. The two women pushed off and floated back to the suit room and docking port.

Richard looked at Ian with a bleary gaze. He had yet to recover from last watch's feast. Ian suspected that he didn't look much better.

"Why don't you stay here with Stasz, as backup?"

"Most gentlemanly of you, my dear professor." He winked at Ian and glided up to Shelley's vacated chair.

Ian pushed off for the open hatchway. As he cleared the doorway he heard a muffled comment and, looking back, saw Richard pass his flask to Stasz.

"For God sake, we're going out to risk our asses and you're soaking it up in here."

Stasz gave a quick smile to Ian, took a pull on the straw, and floated the flask back to its owner.

"Steadies me nerves, it does," he said with an absurd brogue.

"If you need to go in there and get us out," Ian shouted indignantly, "I don't want a couple of drunks responsible for saving my life."

"I'm insulted, my overly righteous friend," Richard replied. "This doesn't sound like the comrade of my happier youth. Why, you're becoming too official, Ian Lacklin."

With a miffed expression Richard turned away to gaze out at the docking bay, which was lining up in the center of the viewport.

"Idiots," Ian muttered, and continued aft to join the women.

"Port seals secured, Ian. You can open it up at your discretion."

"Right. Stasz, stand by if we need any help." He tried to detect any sign of drunkenness in the pilot's voice, but so far nothing.

Ian looked back at Ellen and Shelley. "Ready?"

They floated side by side at the back end of the chamber. Shelley, of course, could barely contain her eagerness. Hell, maybe he should let her pop the door while he hid back there with Ellen. He was almost tempted to do it, but what little male chauvinism he possessed forced him to lead the way.

"You both have the specs on this unit. Given its founding philosophy, if anyone is alive, we should find some interesting results."

They nodded silently, and he knew that a nightmare image was hovering in Ellen's mind. It floated in his consciousness, as well.

Ian punched up the control panel command and the airlock hatch slid back, revealing the colony's door on the other side. It was lightly pitted by micrometeor impacts, but the old Anglo-American writing and instructions were still clearly visible. He double-checked the procedure, took hold of the handles, and braced his feet in the magnetic footholds that Stasz had installed. With one sharp pull, the doorway silently opened and a *whoosh* of air whistled past him. Instinctively he closed his eyes and braced for another nightmare. Nothing touched him; finally he opened his eyes and looked around.

The vessel's airlock chamber was empty. Pushing off, Ian and the two women drifted into the narrow room. Ellen turned and fumbled with the hatch mechanism, securing the vessel from the outside.

She gave Ian the go-ahead. Taking a deep breath, he popped the next door, which opened onto the main docking chamber. The room was dimly lit by translucent panels, and a quick scan told him that the chamber had not been maintained or entered in years.

The vast majority of light panels were dark, and all were covered with a thin coating of dust.

"Must be running on automatic," Shelley whispered.

"If my Old English spelling is good," Ellen interrupted, "I believe that sign over there points us to the main chamber."

Following Ellen's lead, they soon faced a large circular doorway at the end of the corridor.

"This is the end of the nonrotational shaft," Ian said, "assuming, of course, that the blueprints are correct. We clear this door and then enter the main rotating cylinder. Be careful as you go through, you'll be a hundred and fifty meters up from the floor. If you push off too rapidly, you'll float out into the center and it will be a pain to get you back. Just grab hold of the handrails and start to pull yourself down. Watch how I do it."

"Tell me, Dr. Lacklin," Ellen interjected with a playful touch of malice, "how much experience have you had doing this sort of thing?"

"None," he whispered, trying to cover the rush of fear.

He pulled the door release, and as it started to slide open, he felt a moment of panic. But the hatch slid quietly back and there was a barely perceptible rush of air as the pressure equalized. Ian gulped and pushed out.

It was stunning; beyond his wildest imaginings . . . and he was terrified.

The cylinder stretched on for nearly a kilometer, verdant with lush semitropical growth. Broad bands of green alternated with narrow fields of black, through which the reflected images of the stars shone in blazing intensity. Illumination came from the opposite end of the cylinder, where a battery of lights emitted a soft yellow glow that bathed the world in a gentle late-afternoon light. He looked down as he drifted out the doorway and a squeal of terror burst from his lips. He had the sensation of falling and the wild vertigo turned his stomach upside down. The network of handhold cables were all around him and in desperation he snagged hold of one and hung on for dear life.

Laughing, Shelley came up and grabbed hold alongside of him.

"Do as you do, Dr. Lacklin," Shelley said teasingly, and she pushed herself off the handhold and drifted over to the stairs that spiraled down along the cylinder wall. He started to follow her.

Within the first fifty feet he started to detect a faint sense of gravity, but Shelley still continued in a headdown direction, as if diving toward the ground.

"Not too fast, Shelley," Ian called, as if advising an overzealous child, "it can be deceiving. Gravity will pick up significantly the farther we are from the center of rotation."

He looked straight up and noticed that Ellen was coming down feet first, still holding on to the handrailings. He liked the fact that she was frightened; somehow it made his own fear more palatable.

They passed the fifty-meter marker and now even Shelley was feet down and using the steps. She was taking ten steps at a bound, but at least she was slowing down.

"Ian, look at that."

Ellen had stopped at the fifty-meter observation platform. He suddenly realized that she had followed the right course of action. They all should have observed the situation carefully before barging down to the cylinder floor.

"What is it?"

"First off, none of the structures down there seems occupied, they're all overgrown. Second, I've yet to see a person. But third, look up overhead and about halfway down the cylinder."

Ian leaned his head back and gazed up to where she was pointing. It was a shock to see the greenness directly above them, where a lifetime of conditioning had taught him that the sky should be located. He scanned the distant floor for several minutes before finally locating what she had pointed out.

"It looks like smoke."

"Shelley, hold it up for a minute." He looked down and saw that she was continuing on.

"Shelley!"

She stopped, looked back up, and tapped the side of her helmet to signal there was something wrong with her transceiver. Ian gestured for her to hold, but she turned and kept on going.

"She's full of crap," Ellen muttered.

"I know. Call it youthfulness. Something that you and I, my dear Ellen, have started to leave behind."

"Maybe you, Doctor."

"All right, Ellen, all right, let's not get into an argument."

He fell silent and looked out over the expanse of green that had run riot through the ship. His gaze drifted back up toward the smoke. Was it smoke or condensation venting from a broken pipe? And where were the people? The system was still running, almost the entire ship could be programmed to go on automatic, but certain routine repairs definitely required human intervention.

"Shall we go back up the other way and investigate the smoke?" Ellen ventured.

"Seems a logical place to start."

He looked over the railing for Shelley, but she was nowhere in sight.

"Say, look, Shelley," Ian started, "don't give me that crap about a bad radio. If we get back into the ship and I discover it to be working, I'm going to kick your butt."

He stopped for a moment. An image of Shelley's backside flashed in his mind and suddenly, for the first time, it was an appealing backside. Naw, must be the isolation of three months out, Ian thought.

"Shelley!"

His voice was suddenly cut off by a loud, piercing scream.

"Ian!"

"Shelley, what the hell is going on!"

"Ian!"

"Shelley. Shelley, what the hell?"

There was no response.

"Ian, down there to the left." Ellen was pointing into the heavy growth, and Ian saw the canopy of brush moving as if something were passing underneath it.

"Ian, this is Stasz. What the hell is going on? That girl of yours nearly busted my eardrums."

"I don't know, I just don't know..." His voice tapered off. This is what he had feared from the start. The responsibility so far had been merely to point out a direction or, at worst, to mediate fights between the team members. But in his deepest fears he had dreaded this moment. Someone was in jeopardy and he had to decide. Worse. He had to got into what was obviously a dangerous situation.

He stood frozen by the railing watching the overgrowth ripple toward the middle of the cylinder. He wished more than anything to be absolved, to suddenly disappear back to his little cubbyhole in the stern of the *Discovery* where he could hide away with his books and forget.

"Ian!" Several voices called at once, all cutting in, demanding. Vaguely he looked at Ellen and saw her mouth moving behind her faceplate, shouting at him in exasperation.

"Ian, we're coming over," Stasz said. A grunt of assertion surfaced from Richard.

The words started to form in his throat: "Yes, come over and find her, I'm going back to the ship." But that's not what came out.

"Stay there, by the time you suit up they'll be gone. Ellen, go back for a stun gun, I'll try to follow."

He pushed off from the platform, descending the steps in long lazy bounds with each jump landing slightly harder than the one before. He had to be careful not to push off too enthusiastically, otherwise it would be one long jump to the bottom, with an impact at killing velocity. He suddenly remembered some of the cheap space thrillers he had witnessed on the videos, where strange radiation-laden mutants preyed on extraordinarily buxom young nubiles. He actually chuckled at the thought. Shelley was flat-chested, acned, skinny, and bespectacled—he had never seen a monster eat anyone like that before.

What the hell was he laughing at? Maybe that crap was true after all. Ian reached the bottom of the stairs and was confronted by a wild tangle of growth. A virtual jungle canopied the living units and turned the designed green-spaces into nearly impenetrable wildernesses. Ian recognized the plant as a variation of the kudzo, which still flourished in the south and had been used aboard the colonies as a quick-growing greenery and food source.

He soon found a number of broken branches, then another broken branch, ten feet farther on. There appeared to be a tunnel. He surveyed it cautiously for several long minutes, and even as he looked at it, he suddenly realized that the cylinder was getting darker.

"Ellen, are you still up there?"

"No, I'm back in the ship getting the stun gun. Stasz will be coming back with me."

"The lights are shutting down." He felt a chill. His

mind raced over the fact and then the obvious answer came to him. Even here, a thousand years out, the old custom of day and night remained. The unit's artificial sun was shutting down. Well, if he was going to find Shelley, he had to push on.

Taking a deep breath, he started into the tunnel. "I'm entering a tunnel about fifty feet from the base of the stairs. It seems to run along a walkway now overgrown, you'll see the broken branches."

He broke into a slow run, but within a hundred yards he had overtaxed the cooling system of his suit and his own body.

Hell, why am I wearing his pressure cooker? Those plants are oxygen producers, I should crack the helmet.

But the old Ian was still very much alive—he kept the helmet on while contemplating the toxic trace elements that could have filtered into the closed environment.

After several more minutes the twilight seemed to darken appreciably, and against his better judgment Ian turned on his helmet light to follow the trail. He knew that it was a clear beacon of warning, but he wasn't up to crawling through the dark.

He passed a spidery walk that gently arched over a complex of glass-walled buildings, all of them covered by the everpresent kudzo. He estimated that he was nearing the center of the cylinder.

He stopped for a moment to look back through a break in the canopy of foliage. The far cylinder wall was visible, and he saw twin specks of light suddenly appear against it.

"Ellen? Stasz? I think I can see you."

"Ian, where are you?"

"About halfway into the cylinder."

"I'm facing you right now, you should be able to see my helmet light."

From atop their high perch, Stasz suddenly saw the flicker of light, a long way off.

"I think I see you, Ian. Say, Ian, I see something else. It looks like a fire, can't be more than a couple of hundred meters beyond you."

There was no response.

"Ian. Ian?"

He looked at Ellen.

"His light just disappeared," Ellen whispered.

"Oh, shit."

"Holy shit," Ian whispered.

The club was poised alongside his head. The semiclad woman holding it had already convinced him of the need to remove his helmet by her vigorous hand motions and waves of the knotted cudgel. He took a deep breath of the clean-smelling air. Why the hell had he kept that damn helmet on anyhow?

"What do you say?" the woman asked softly, and as she spoke several of her companions came out of the shadows.

Ian sifted through her speech pattern. It seemed to be based on Old English, to be sure, actually Old American, to be more precise. As his mind searched for the right words, his thoughts calmed down. He was engaged in an academic problem and when lost to such efforts, all else was forgotten.

"Oly hit?" the woman asked questioningly.

"No, holy shit," Ian repeated slowly.

"Shit is not holy, only the light is holy; you must be crazy." The others around her chuckled.

"Yeah, I think I am for even being here," Ian replied.

"What you say?"

"Never mind."

"Are you of the Dissenters?" a lanky, graying man asked, stepping from out of the shadows.

"What the hell are Dissenters?" Ian replied.

"He must be crazy," a heavyset man next to the graying one interjected.

"You dressed like that loud-mouthed girl. She of your circle?" the woman asked.

"Yeah, ahh, yeah, the girl, she's of my circle."

"Tell me, friend, do you accept the concept that individual meditation must occur within a collective body?" the gray one asked. "Or do you accept the right of dissent from the collective?"

Think quick, Ian, he thought frantically. However, he instinctively realized that twenty years of academic combat and bullshitting had put him in good stead. Ian noticed how the graying one said dissent with a note of venom. He also realized that the gray man held a very big club.

"What say you, friend?" the heavyset one asked softly, and he slowly hefted his club.

"Of course, what other way is there?" Ian blurted. "The individual must always be a part within the collective body." He prayed that he got his words correct; most of the Old American was familiar, but occasional colloquialism and, of course, the slang could be deadly. Especially now, so he tried to speak with rigid preciseness.

He could sense them relaxing.

"Come, friend, and sit with us in the circle of understanding." The woman beckoned for him to follow.

She looked at him with a soft glow, and he suddenly realized how attractive she was in a wild, primitive way. She was almost completely naked except for a brief loincloth that barely covered her broad, inviting hips. He couldn't help but admire her full, rounded breasts, which were partially concealed by her flowing red hair. She noticed his stare and smiled back at him with a seductive gaze. For the moment thoughts of rescue drifted away.

Primitives, he thought, looking for all the world like Neolithic tribesmen or something out of Eden. Yes, it could be Eden: the lush growth, the warm semitropical air, and now that the helmet was off, the sounds of birds and night creatures stirring around him.

Following the lead of the woman, they pushed their

way into a small clearing, illuminated by a roaring blaze. Several dozen figures sat around the crackling flame, and one of them was Shelley.

He couldn't help but look at the redhead, even as he tried to get his thoughts under control. Shelley turned as one of the people by the fire pointed at the new arrivals.

"Shelley, everything, all right?"

"Ian? Well, if it isn't Dr. Lacklin, who's finally come to rescue me."

Was she mocking him, or was there a slight tone of relief in her voice?

Ian stepped into the circle of light and, gazing around, saw that dozens more had gathered around in curiosity.

He drifted over to Shelley's side, smiling broadly and nervously all the while, noticing that they smiled back just as broadly. Good lord, why are they smiling like such damn fools at a total stranger?

"Dinner." Someone was poking him in the back.

He turned with a yelp and was confronted by an old man bent over with age.

"Dinner," the man said again.

Good lord, was that why they were smiling? They were going to have them for dinner.

"Shelley!"

"It's okay, Ian, the food's not bad. Some sort of vegetarian mix, that's all."

He finally understood and broke into a nervous grin. "Thank you, ahh, friend."

A number of people around the circle mumbled their approval at his comment.

He drew closer to Shelley and sat down by her side. "What happened?"

"Most likely, same as you. They jumped me, but once I took the helmet off, they calmed down. Something about dissenters and I assured them I was nothing of the sort, and after that everything was fine. They brought me back here, fed me some broth, then you came in."

The old man brought over a wooden plate filled with a thick white soup. Ian took a hesitant sip, remembering all of his anthropological studies about primitive societies and eating rituals. The woman he admired earlier stepped out of the crowd and sat by his side.

"You from Earth, or another colony?"

This was a surprise. He expected some mumbo jumbo about gods from other worlds, or some similar nonsense.

"Earth. How did you guess that?"

"We're not stupid. You obviously aren't from here, at least not dressed like that."

"But how do you know about Earth? Did your elders teach you or—"

"Come now," she admonished, and lightly touched him on the arm, a move that Shelley could not fail to notice. "We do not understand everything, but some of the teaching computers and their programs still work. When we're young we use them."

"If you can do that, then why do you?..."

"You mean, live like primitives. Why not? Maybe you should ask yourself that."

"Yes, friend," another woman interjected, "why not live like primitives?"

"But how do you keep your system running?"

"Most of it was automated by our forefathers. All we have to do is routine maintenance, which is simple."

"Which frees us of the slavery of complexity, so that we can return to simplicity and light," another one said, and a chorus of voices murmured in the affirmative. Ian looked up and noticed that several hundred people had gathered around the roaring fire.

"They're just getting started," Shelley whispered.

"When we foreswear complexity, then all is balanced," a young man said from the back of the crowd. "Then and only then is true simplicity obtained."

This is crazy, Ian thought, what are we getting into, first-year philosophy?

"But the order of your world is built on complexity," Ian tried cautiously.

"But we have purified it back to the basics," another replied.

"However, you live in one of the most complex machines ever designed by man. Once you accept that first step toward complexity, there is no going back."

"But we have," several replied eagerly.

"As I said," Shelley whispered, "don't even try."

"But this is a machine you live in, not Eden," Ian replied, "and a machine requires technical skills. Just suppose something really serious should go wrong."

"Nothing has, and nothing will," the redhead replied. "We have everything under control, as long as we follow the simplicity of collective meditation and consensus."

"Tell me more about the dissenters," Shelley asked, wishing to extract Ian from a potentially dangerous debate. Ian, however, shot her a quick look of reproach. These people obviously got excited, a little too excited, about the dissenters. He still wasn't sure if he and Shelley were guests or prisoners, and until he knew more, he wanted to keep them smiling.

"They are the ones who fell," the gray-bearded elder replied.

"How so?" Shelley continued.

"Can't you yourself see their folly?"

Oh, no, Ian thought, step carefully.

"Look out! Incoming!"

A wild explosion of confusion erupted. The people scattered in every direction, screaming in terror. For a second Ian thought Shelley had triggered something and they were now going to be ripped apart. Then he noticed the colonists were all running away, and he wondered if he and Shelley had broken some taboo, which caused them to flee.

A roaring, *whish*ing noise thundered overhead.

"What the hell!" Ian felt something brush past his

shoulder and for an instant thought Shelley was pressing up against him.

"Ian?"

"Yeah." He turned to look at her. But his view was now blocked. A huge arrow, nearly a dozen feet in length and as thick around as his thigh, was buried in the ground between them. The pressure on his shoulder came from the still-quivering bolt.

The locals looked at him in open-mouthed amazement. He tried a wan smile of bravado, wishing for a quick line. Ian looked back at the arrow, its heavy point buried only inches away from his foot. His eyes rolled up and he fainted dead away.

He heard a roaring sound, as if he were trapped in a waterfall. The shouting was all around him, and the individual voices soon came clear.

"Those sons of bitches!"

There was a wild frenzy of activity. Shelley had dragged him off to one side of the circle.

"Another incoming!"

The crowd scattered and this time he noticed that most of them disappeared into the vine-covered buildings that surrounded the clearing. He saw the bolt streaking in, following a strange curving trajectory. The arrow slammed against the side of a building and shattered.

"Bastards, ass-kissing Dissenters." The crowd poured out of the buildings, chanting.

"Bastards, bastards, bastards." The air around them pulsed with a rippling energy. From out of the shadows an object out of ancient history was dragged by an enthusiast mob.

"Double torsion ballista," Ian murmured. The urge of the historian was too much. He crawled out from under the protection of the building and went over and joined the shouting mob.

He walked up close to the machine. It was the real

thing, and he felt a rippling thrill. The twin bundles of rope that powered it were made of human hair, while the bowstring appeared to be made of steel cable. Half a dozen young women carried up a ten-foot arrow and the crowd roared with pleasure at the sight.

The machine was cocked by hand-powered windlasses then tilted back so that it pointed halfway up to vertical.

What the hell? Ian stepped back. Why were they shooting an arrow straight up?

The crowd suddenly fell silent, and suddenly he heard a soft echoing chant.

"Assholes, assholes, assholes."

He looked around wondering where the distant chanting came from, until Shelley touched his shoulder and pointed straight up.

"Look."

Ian tilted his head back and then he suddenly remembered. They had seen another fire on the opposite side of the cylinder. Directly overhead and three hundred meters away was the other side, and a flickering fire illuminated the sky above them in a soft ruddy glow.

Ian sidled up alongside the redhead. He gulped as he came closer. The exertion and excitement had covered her body with a sheen of sweat, and her eyes were wild with excitement that had a most definite sexual aura to it.

He collected his thoughts and pointed straight up. "Dissenters?"

She nodded her head vigorously.

The graybeard took up position alongside the catapult, which was now loaded, and grabbed hold of the trigger.

"We are the truth," he intoned. "Therefore in the name of the truth and the light we are absolved of this action. It is not my hand that triggers this, it is the result of our consensus, therefore I am not responsible, for the consensus makes me do it. But it is moral nevertheless, since we are right."

"We are right and they are wrong," the crowd roared.

"Fuck you" came a distant reply.

The elder yanked the trigger.

The catapult snapped with a thunderous crack. The arrow leaped away into the dark.

Ian was amazed. "Say, I thought I read somewhere that you were founded by believers in peace?"

"But we *are* followers of peace."

"That looks like a weapon of war to me."

"No, it's not, it's random luck. We don't aim it at anyone, if they get hit it's the will of a higher power. We believe in peace more than they do, and we are right, therefore our protest against them is for the higher cause of peace."

He tried to follow the logic but gave up.

"It's going to be a long night," the redhead whispered, drawing closer, and her hand lightly touched his side.

"But it looks like you people are having a war here," Ian said weakly. "How can we? I mean, aren't they going to come down and attack...?"

"No, that would be violence. They stay on their side, we stay on ours, and we trade spears. What do you think, we're savages or something?"

She drew closer, her naked breasts brushing against his arm.

He didn't dare to answer.

As he stepped out of the building into the soft diffused light of day, Ian felt a sense of guilt. Shelley sat by the ashes of the fire, notepad in hand, punching in observations. He ambled over to her side feeling rather sheepish.

"So, tell me, are primitive mating customs all they're cracked up to be? Shelley told us what you were up to in there."

It was Ellen! He turned around and there on the opposite side of the square stood Stasz and Ellen. Ellen's expression was definitely not one of cheerful good morning.

The redhead came out of the shelter, raised her arms up over her head, and stretched with a supple feline grace. Ellen's expression reddened, and on Stasz's there was genuine admiration as he kept looking from the girl and back to Ian. She smiled a vague sort of hello in their direction, then wandered off into the overgrowth. Shelley didn't even look up but simply continued with her notes.

"I'm glad to see you were in good hands and safe," Ellen snarled. "We wandered over half this god damn botanical toilet looking for you. Then we get captured by those, what did they call themselves, 'true dissenters,' and then . . ."

"Watch what you say," Shelley snapped.

"Are you addressing me?" Ellen purred, getting ready to strike.

"I would suggest that if you are referring to our friends up there"—Shelley pointed vaguely toward the other side—"that you do so quietly. And for God's sake, don't call them true dissenters. Our friends around here get upset rather easily."

Ellen knew she couldn't argue with her, but Ian and Stasz could see that Shelley had insulted her by pointing out something she should have realized already.

As if in response, a faint drifting call echoed down from above. "Collectivist assholes!"

"Oh, no, here we go again." Ian groaned.

"Naw, they're too exhausted," Shelley replied. "It was a hell of a night."

"To be sure," Stasz said, his voice edged with jealousy as he looked back in the direction the redhead had taken.

A couple of men were still gathered around the catapult, which was loaded, and Ian could see this would be the last shot of the fray, since everyone had gone off to sleep. The old graybeard, however, was still up and directing the alignment of the siege engine.

"Gates, the old graybeard, is the leader. By the way, you might like to know that you spent the night with his daughter Ileia," Shelley said softly.

Ian looked at his feet and muttered a comment about observing local customs.

"Gates filled me in on some fascinating details," Shelley continued, ignoring his embarrassment. "I've recorded them all, Dr. Lacklin, so that you may study them later, when you feel up to it."

Stasz snickered and turned away, while Ian tried to come up with a casual reply.

"Freethinker bastards!" It was Gates and one of his followers.

"Watch this," Shelley said.

The catapult hurled its shot, which arced up and away. It followed an arching path, due to the Coriolis effect created by the turning of the cylinder. In the daylight Ian now realized that the catapult was not aimed straight at the other campsite but a good sixty degrees off.

He watched the bolt climb in a curving path—at least it appeared that way. As it reached toward the relative apogee in the center, the bolt slowed, then with ever-increasing speed it started the long sloping glide back down.

"Pretty good accuracy," Shelley said, "considering the physics of shooting an arrow inside a turning cylinder."

Ian watched with admiration as the bolt streaked in and landed near the bull's-eyelike target created by the dissenters' campfire. There was a mild scurrying and he half imagined that he could see several people look up and shake their fists.

"You missed me" came the taunting cry from the other side.

"The forms these people are going to fill out will be fascinating," Ellen whispered.

Gates and his two assistants shook their fists at the

other side, and calling it quits, they went into the nearest building to catch up on their sleep.

Ian looked around the cylinder, at least able to get a good chance to observe his environment without the pressure of looking for Shelley. Its scale was truly astounding, but what amazed Ian even more was the realization that this was a small unit of early design. There were colonial cylinders of the same general design that were fifty times as big in volume. He looked up again at the lovely sweep of green overgrowth that covered nearly everything. He wondered how the unit managed to allow so much of its carbon and nitrogen to be fixed in such a profusion of plants, but then from his own rough estimate the population here must only be a few percentile points of the bearing capacity. So that great percentage no longer in existence must be a fair part of the liquid and other materials tied up in the unit. The thought suddenly struck him with chilling force. Back on Earth one could not easily grasp the total cyclic nature of life. He once had a prof who pointed out that, statistically speaking, the next glass of water you drank would be carrying in it a molecule from Caesar's body—and from Cleopatra's urine, one of his classmates had rudely interjected.

But here the system was closer. These people, Gates, Ileia, a good part of their very bodies were made up of the component chemicals that had formed their grandsires before the coming of the Holocaust.

As a historian the thought awed him. But there was a more overriding concern at the moment. He was simply exhausted.

"I'm heading back to the ship. If you people stay, I would suggest that you do so as a group. I'll send Richard down to take a look at these people."

"I take it we're staying for a while?" Shelley asked.

"Well, I guess that's what we've come sixty light-years for. We'll stay a week or so to gather the necessary data, document this place, then we'll push on."

"I want to get my surveys out," Ellen said excitedly. "This is going to be fascinating. I should get at least two or three publications out of this one."

"And I think I'll get something, as well," Stasz said eagerly, as he edged off to one side of the group and then turned to plunge into the overgrowth.

"I'm going back to sleep aboard ship. I don't want any of these people allowed aboard the vessel," Ian commanded. "If both sides met there, we would be the ones to suffer. So they stay out. I would suggest that we get Stasz to rig up a simple security surveillance system on the approaches to the air lock."

"I'll let him know when he gets back," Shelley said.

Ian turned and started back up the path. He gave a quick scan up, looking for incoming. Their catapult was visible but it was unattended.

"Get some rest, Dr. Lacklin," Shelley called. "You've had a hard night."

He looked back at Shelley. She had that straight, official look about her, all professional.

"Ah, yeah, thanks, Shelley." He searched awkwardly for words, "Yes. You did a good job."

"I doubt if you did." Ellen sniffed.

"Ah, shut up," Ian grumbled, and he pushed off back to the ship.

"All secured for undocking," Stasz's voice crackled over the intercom.

Ian felt the gentle nudge of the ship as the maneuvering thrusters pushed them free and away.

He watched on the aft monitor as the bulk of the cylinder dropped astern.

"I still think they're the craziest assholes I've ever laid eyes on," Richard said, resuming their conversation.

"Don't say assholes, Richard," Ellen replied, "I've heard that word shouted at least ten thousand times in the last two weeks."

"Okay, bastards."

"Richard!"

"I'm throttling up," Stasz said. A faint pulsing rumble echoed through the ship and the slight tug of gravity increased. Funny, he barely noticed the gravity changes anymore, and his stomach couldn't be in better shape.

"That's one group I'm glad to be rid of," Richard muttered as he uncapped a beaker of gin and offered it around. Even Ellen took a quick snort and smiled her gratitude.

"So damned self-righteous, both of them," Shelley replied. "I still can't figure out what split them up." She looked to Ellen, their sociologist who was always ready with a theory.

"I don't know, some doctrinal point about their worship service. I think the break came nearly a millennium ago. Fascinating how they ritualized their war. They never engaged in direct killing close up, they clearly defined their boundaries and observed them, and I found at least one record in their computer that indicated they had cooperated when the vessel was holed. They even cooperated in their birth reductions and contraceptives to maintain the low population. But Lord, did they get into symbolic warfare."

"It sure as hell didn't look symbolic to me," Richard replied. "Thank heavens those crazies didn't have a couple of small thermonukes; they'd have wiped each other out long ago. What do you think, Ian? Ian?"

Ian sat off to one side, his expression pale as he fumbled with his pockets. But the others barely noticed as Shelley jumped back into the conversation.

"But it was symbolic. It was their catharsis; they could vent their feelings and only occasionally would some unwary person get slammed."

"I still think they were damn fools," Richard muttered, and Shelley nodded her agreement. Ian noticed how she stared at him, and felt a sudden flush of embarrassment.

"I think I'll go forward and watch jump from Stasz's Co seat."

He fumbled through his pockets one more time, but he already knew that what he was looking for was somewhere back on the colony, most likely having fallen from his pocket while he had been "playing" with Ileia. He had mislaid the *Thermomine Manual* and chances were the inhabitants were already pouring through it. He could only hope the symbolic warfare would stay symbolic. He cursed himself soundly; here was yet another thing to feel guilt over, but there was no way he could tell his comrades about this screw up—Ellen would be all over him in a flash.

As Ian closed the door, Ellen was waxing enthusiastic over the data she had collected about controlled primitive societies and ritualized warfare. She had been so enthusiastic that Ian had half expected her to request that she could stay behind, and only a promise of a return visit on their way back home had finally convinced her to leave.

He was half tempted to stay there, as well; Ileia haunted his thoughts. But in a way he was glad that they had decided to pull out. At forty-two he just couldn't keep up with the demands of a healthy eighteen-year-old, no matter how much he would fantasize about her later.

The decision to leave had come as a mild surprise to everyone. They had settled in nicely, learned to dodge the spears, and in fact were even starting to view the war as a great game—as they freely drifted between the two sides, taking notes and observing. Gates had hooked him into the computer log. The records of their initial departure over a millennium ago were still intact—a historical find that would keep dozens of graduate assistants busy for years. There were even fragments of a library and Ian found hundreds of volumes and documents thought to be long lost.

Ian had holed up in there for a week, taking all meals, sleeping only when exhaustion had set in, and pushing off Ileia's advances. And he discovered two disturbing facts.

The first, that a large exile colony had been established for political refugees. He already knew that, and knew as well that it had been the final domain of Dr. Franklin Smith, a noted political dissident in the years just before the Holocaust. He had assumed that Smith's colony had been destroyed when the war started, since the records back home indicated for some vague reason that the unit had died.

It had not.

The records in *Unit 27's* main library indicated a sighting of it some forty years after departure, but their trajectory was faster and Smith's unit had passed them without direct contact.

But it was the second fact that had caused Ian to pull up stakes and leave the peace movement colony behind. Ian had discovered the name of Smith's ship. *Alpha/ Omega*. A strange compulsion was forming in Ian's mind. Even as the compulsion formed it frightened him, for it implied a danger he would rather not face. But for some reason beyond his understanding, he wanted to discover why a colony started by a hero out of the distant past would now engage in wholesale murder. What was it that the poet from *Unit 181* was warning him against? To the surprise of everyone else, Ian had talked them back to the *Discovery* and then immediate departure.

He couldn't understand his own compulsion and tried to make believe that it was a simple intellectual exercise. Even as he pondered this fact, Ian reached the front cabin and swung into the seat alongside of Stasz.

"Proper trajectory set and locked in," Stasz said.

"We're ready."

"Remember those odds, Ian my friend. This jump could be the disintegration act."

Ian didn't reply. Logically they should head back to Earth, report their findings, and let someone else go out and look. But the way the bureaucracy ran, that could take years. And besides, he was starting to find the whole adventure compelling. Challenge was here. And mystery. His mind wandered around that thought even as Stasz pushed them through jump and the wave of distortion washed over him, plunging him into darkness.

CHAPTER 7

Colonial Unit 287

First Completion Date: 2052

Primary Function: Experimental Longevity Unit. Combined Russo/American effort with cybernetic implants designed to continue life beyond the then 130-year maximum. Such research had been banned on Earth in 2041 by the United Nations as a response to Third World pressures concerning the question of population control. Anyone already using artificial organ implants was exiled to space in 2050, with most moving to the 280-model units.

Evacuation Date: December 2085.

Overall Design: Bernal Sphere. Lower rotation rate with .3 G standard gravity. Extensive living area in the zero-G regions.

Propulsion: Matter/Antimatter mix.

Course: Galactic Core.

Political/Social Orientation: Corporate model managed by ruling board. This unit was a nonpolitical interface between the Americans and the Soviets, and yet another example of their expanding cooperation in the middle twenty-first century.

"*Discovery*, you are cleared for final approach and docking."

Stasz had them lined up on the long axis of the slowly rotating sphere, and with gentle nudges of the thruster controls he guided *Discovery* toward the main external docking bay. They had been invited to enter via the main interior bay, but Ian insisted on an outside dock so they could leave whenever they desired and, if need be, without hindrance or permission.

As the massive bulk of the two-kilometer-diameter sphere filled their forward viewscreen, Ian was finally torn from his observations by Shelley's insistent nudge.

"Here's a brief review of the records in your file, I thought you'd like to take them with us. I've provided copies to Richard and Ellen, as well."

"Thanks, shall we join them?"

Shelley nodded her agreement and together they floated down the corridor to the docking bay.

Damn, she's simply too efficient at times, Ian thought. He always felt uncomfortable around efficient people, they made him feel foolish and somewhat guilty. He knew his dallying with Ileia bothered her, but Shelley was only his graduate assistant. Richard had commented time and again over the last ten days 'Remember that virginal graduate assistant of yours is only three years older than your redheaded Amazon.'

Naw, there can't be anything in it. Shelley's a gawky grad-ass with a mild dose of hero worship for her brilliant professor ... He pushed the thought aside; they came through the airlock and joined the other two.

"You've had a chance to scan my notes?" Ian asked.

"Looks fascinating," Ellen replied. "What've they dis-

covered if their experiments have been continued since
their departure?"

"We'll soon know," Richard murmured expectantly as
a faint jolt ran through the ship. The docking adapter
hooked on to the colony's exterior airlock and quickly
formed a pressurized seal.

"All clear," Stasz called from the control room.

Ian reached out and pushed the door release. It slid
back noiselessly. Even as their hatch opened, the colony's
hatch parted, as well, to reveal the usual double-entry
system

Ian and the others pushed off, and as the last of them
cleared the second doorway, it slid shut behind them.

"Dr. Lacklin," said the voice of the colony's approach
control, "as I mentioned earlier, we do request disinfection."

"I doubt if that is necessary," Richard replied.

"Use our disinfection facilities or leave us, Dr. Lacklin."

Ian looked at the others, shrugged. They put on safety
glasses as requested and were dosed with an ultraviolet
bath, followed by a disinfectant spray. Finally they were
required to don robes, surgical masks, and gloves.

Richard looked professional in the robes, but Ellen
snickered at the sight of the old M.D. as he flapped around
in zero G wrapped in a green hospital gown.

"We're ready," Ian called. The second doorway opened.
The slight inrush of air carried the scent of disinfectant
and alcohol, mixed with a slightly unpleasant *something*
that made all of them feel uneasy.

They exited into the main corridor, where a slender
man floated in free-fall. Ian had wondered what he would
look like. He had expected a bent form, aged beyond
imagining, dried out, his desiccated flesh fit only for the
grave. But this one was different. He was old, extremely
old. If anything gave the age away, it was the eyes that
betrayed a soul that had seen too much. The man was

totally bald; the skin of his head wrinkled and yellow like old parchment. But he moved with an easy grace as he floated closer, his robes rustling lightly and giving off a scent of cleanness and starch.

"I am Joshua Morisson," the man said with a crisp voice that was almost too precise and clear, "and you must be Drs. Lacklin, Croce, and Redding." He nodded to each in turn.

He stared at Shelley for a moment and smiled softly. "And you are their young assistant Shelley."

His smile flickered and then died. "You have much to tell me, all of you. I want to hear again of Earth."

Ian looked at him closely, almost afraid to ask.

"I want to hear again of my home," Joshua whispered, "for you see, Dr. Lacklin, I am over sixty-score years of age. And I wish again to hear of the world where I was young."

The others were gone, off on a tour of the colony, led by an assistant who looked even older than Joshua. But Ian had not wanted to leave the man. Here was the dream of a lifetime fulfilled at last. He stood face to face with a life that had spanned a millennium, a life that had seen that distant time of so long ago when the world was young—and the greatest of adventures was just beginning.

So he had answered with patience the old man's questions and watched with fascination as his host explored the corridors of long-forgotten memories. Occasionally the old man softly cried, as if each of the memories was a sharpened point driven into his psyche, reopening long-forgotten wounds.

"So, it is all gone—Washington, London, Moscow, the great museums, the lovely churches, the soaring monuments—all gone, as lost now as Troy and Carthage."

"Not really," Ian replied. "There is a New Mosca and

Nova Washington. I participated at a dig for the old Capitol building when I was a graduate student."

Joshua nodded sadly. "You see, young Ian. You see. You participated in a 'dig,' as you call it, for something that is still alive in my mind. You were digging for relics where I walked when I was a boy. I remember"—and his voice grew softer—"I remember seeing a President buried out of that Capitol when I was seven."

"Who?" Ian's curiosity was screaming at him. Here was the link. The living memory that could touch back into a long-lost world. It was the ultimate dream come true. This man had been there, had seen, had experienced it all—ten thousand questions begged to be answered.

"Who? Who? Why I'm not sure," Joshua said softly. "I can see him, I can remember his voice carrying clear and high on a cold January day, and then he was dead. But who was he, you ask." His voice drifted away.

Ian waited patiently, hoping that the layers of memory would be stirred, but nothing came, just a slight shaking of the head and then a half-bemused smile of sadness.

"It is so long ago that I have not thought of it in a hundred, maybe two hundred years. I am old, Ian, my comrades and I. Old as if we were like Adam, bent under the weight of endless centuries since the loss of Paradise."

Ian leaned forward and touched Joshua on the hand. He felt a sense of awe that he was touching something alive from the distant age he had dreamed about since childhood. He realized, as well, that underneath this "specimen" that he wished to probe and record, there was a man like himself. "How does it feel?" Ian whispered. "I somehow can't imagine it—how does it feel to have lived so long?"

Joshua smiled, as if he had waited and prepared for that question. "I can remember when I was a child. There was a thing called movies, do you have them still?"

Ian nodded.

"I can remember a day when I wanted to go to a movie

and my mother said she would take me that afternoon into the city. How I wanted to see it, how I had waited for weeks for that film to arrive. It was early in the morning, and so I settled down to wait for my mother to take me. And the seconds dragged by as if each fragment was a frozen entity slowly melting, to be replaced by yet another slow melting fragment. I waited for an eternity . . ." His voice trailed off for a moment, so that Ian thought he had fallen asleep, but suddenly he stirred.

"Do you remember the eternity of time when you were a child? That morning will be forever frozen in my mind. I believe that only a child can truly see time in its passage. As we grow older time slips through our fingers without our ever grasping it. And now you ask what my eternity is like.

"I will tell you, Ian Lacklin, that the centuries of this endless journey have seemed like but a moment to me, when compared to that morning of a millennium ago. For all of time is an illusion. I drift now through eternity and no longer feel its passage. There is no awe, there is nothing to excite, there is only eternity."

He knew the question was foolish but he had to ask.

"What was the, ahh, movie, I think you called it?"

Joshua smiled again, as if he knew that this question would be asked, as well. "I can't recall now, it was something about the future and our distant past. It was about space and a man who traveled far, but I can't recall. All I remember is that in the end, we didn't go. My mother forgot her promise to me and left with some friends, and so I didn't go. And across the centuries all I can now remember is the pain."

"How have you managed this?" Ian asked. "How have you lived so long?"

"Ahh, how have I kept the spirit trapped in this vessel? I believe you are the historian, Ian, you must know of our grand design?"

"All I have are the few records that survived the Holocaust."

"So that is what you call it now. I remember we used that word for something else, as well. But I guess that it is fitting, a burnt offering, yes, that is fitting.

"But you wish to know how, rather than simply to hear the ramblings of an old man."

"They're not ramblings," Ian said softly. "If need be I'll stay here as long as you will allow me, for I am far more interested than you can imagine. Joshua, you are my dream, you lived then, while I can only dream of that time. You saw it with those eyes, and through you I want to see it, as well."

"These eyes, you say." Joshua chuckled softly. "Yes, these eyes. But let me return to your original question as to how."

Ian pointed to his wrist to ask if he could record the conversation. It took Joshua several seconds to realize the nature of the small device on Ian's wrist, but he nodded his approval even as he started to talk.

"I was a genetic engineer, a researcher on the edge of our bold new frontier. And through our research, and in many other realms as well, we felt at last that we could even stare death in the face and turn him back. Our strategies were many, just as a general will employ many different weapons, each appropriate to its task, to win his war. For this indeed was war—we were fighting the greatest tyrant of all.

"Some followed the paths of mechanical engineering, so that it became possible to replace many of the organs that had once been the cause of so much anguish and pain. Soon we had the heart, the liver, the kidney, hormone producers, and even the eyes," and as he said that he gently pointed to his right eye, "which you in error said had witnessed such distant times. But the engineers' victories were merely successful counterattacks; it was we, the bioengineers, the genetic scientists, who turned the tide of victory. We learned cells would only reproduce for so many generations before losing their vitality; we learned to halt that decline in individual cells; we learned, as well, to supply antibodies tailored to the needs of each individual, growing outside his body a reserve specially designed and ready for instant application. We also mastered the rebuilding of major organs by genetic manipulation of individual cells.

"We learned these things, and the world hated us. For our wonders were expensive beyond all imagining. Only the wealthy, only those who had made their fortunes could afford our treatments. And as billions starved, hundreds who had everything learned to extend life, to stare death in the face and cheat him of his prey. So at last the hatred of the world turned against us, and we were banished to space.

"But we already knew that space was the only place we could go to if we truly wished to cheat the final adversary. For on Earth there was too much that killed. Gravity kills as inexorably as any disease. It taxes the body, it exacts payment from its victims. Here there would be no accidents to our bodies that we could not repair, here our environment could be controlled, everything softened, everything designed, everything..."

His words drifted off for a moment.

"We've cheated him," Joshua whispered, "we've cheated him. I can live yet another thousand years and if need be, I can be saved."

"Saved?"

"Yes, many choose that in the end. If something goes wrong that we cannot stop—forms of senility, damage to memory, certain rare cancers that we have yet to learn how to control—we simply save the person. He is placed in suspended animation—ahh, I think the word is hibernation."

"You've mastered that?"

"Yes, in the year that we fled from Earth, before the

war, our researchers found the answers and learned to synthesize the necessary hormones that would trigger that most ancient of protections."

"That is fantastic!" Ian replied. "Richard has to hear about this! It could revolutionize space travel. It could open up the entire universe!"

"Yes, I would have thought your people knew about this; we shared the knowledge with another colony as payment for their leaving us alone. This was just before we left Earth. I would have thought they would have spread the information."

"What colony was that?" Ian asked casually.

"I remember meeting with their leader, he was a student of mine. Funny—he was a reasonable sort of man, but driven. I gave him a small supply of the hormone, and to my surprise, he honored his word and left us. I had thought there for a moment that we would have died after all."

"Who was he?"

"His name was Smith."

Ian wanted to push for more on that, but his thoughts were becoming disoriented, as if he had suddenly been turned round and round. So what if Franklin Smith had been here? More than a millennium had passed, and with it a journey across trillions of miles. But he still felt the haunting image of the poet, floating—his words, a portent of warning.

"Would you like to see the rest?" Joshua whispered.

"What?" He was suddenly pulled back from his thoughts.

"The rest, my old friends, my fellow travelers."

"How many are like you?" Ian asked. "How many were born before the Holocaust?"

"All of us," Joshua replied. "The youngest woman to come aboard was already long past childbearing age. We are all of the long before."

Floating up out of his chair, he gently pushed off toward the doorway and beckoned for Ian to follow.

They passed out of the docking and reception areas and finally entered the main living area of the sphere.

The smell of antiseptic was overwhelming, and with it that faint, unpleasant scent Ian could not quite place. There was a silence to the colony, as if they were in the realm of the dead.

Occasional white-robed figures would float by, and some would nod a greeting to Joshua. Ian soon noticed that very few of the ghostlike people displayed what he thought should be a natural curiosity over a stranger. The colony's inhabitants drifted by as if lost in a dream.

Joshua finally led the way out of the free-float environment, and, boarding an elevator, they rode down to the one-third-gravity level at the base of the sphere.

Joshua walked with obvious discomfort and unsteadiness. This section was almost entirely empty. They slowly walked along a white corridor that looked to Ian to be typical of some early hospital ward.

"Where is everyone?" Ian asked. "I haven't seen anyone since we've come down."

"I'll show you," Joshua replied as they came to a double door that opened silently at their approach.

Ian felt a sudden uneasy compulsion. He wanted to break away from this skeletal figure and run. Run out of the hospital with its nightmarish feel of infirmity and death.

He saw Richard, Ellen, and Shelley standing on the other side of the door, the three of them obviously subdued.

"Ahh, your friends," Joshua said softly. "Dr. Croce, I hope you've found our technology to be of some interest."

Richard nodded slowly but was silent.

Ian's eyes gradually adjusted to the low level of blue lighting, and he recoiled with horror. The nightmare flashed back for a second and he wanted to scream.

They were standing in a long corridor that curved upward and away, and he suddenly realized that this hallway completely circled the ship. And it was packed with bodies.

They were suspended from the ceiling, each one wrapped in a see-through sarcophagus; each sarcophagus was linked with several tubes and monitors to a biosensor.

"Here is our sleep," Joshua whispered, as if afraid that too loud a voice might awaken the sleepers.

"When something finally strikes us that we cannot cure, we take the hormonal injections that trigger our hibernation. Thus we shall ride out the millennium until at last the cures are found, until rejuvenation itself can be re-created, until even we can be made young again."

Ian walked away from Joshua. And stared off aimlessly. The bodies hung around him on either side. All of them old, old and shriveled, yet still alive in their endless sleep journey. To each was affixed a data card, and he quickly scanned some.

JOHN KEENE B. 5-3-1965 HIB. 7-11-2238. ALZ-HEIMERS, RECURRING MALIGNANCY.

ANDREW BARRY B. 7-17-1964 HIB. 8-1-2718. INSAN-ITY.

WILLIAM WEBSTER B. 8-18-1945 HIB. 4-4-2110. IN-SANITY.

Ian looked back at Joshua. All of them born a hundred years before the Holocaust! In their minds were locked the memories. And such memories—memories of a grand and heroic age that he thought was lost. How they must have felt to have been part of the great epic. How they must have been enthralled. But as he looked back at them he also felt a growing sense of uneasiness. And Joshua stood quiet. Watching.

"How many like this?" Ian asked.

"As of yesterday's accounting, 28,455."

Ian turned and started to walk down the corridor, casually glancing at each nameplate.

INSANITY
ALZHEIMERS
ATTEMPTED SUICIDE
SENILITY
INSANITY

"What is happening here?" Ian whispered, as if to himself.

"You know," Joshua said, coming up alongside of Ian, "there are only one thousand fifty of us left—those that are still awake. I find it strange somehow to think of it. We have turned ourselves into a company of sleepers. We have cheated death and will continue to cheat him across all eternity, as we fly through the night—forever running. But eternity itself is a trap. We have cheated it. But still it exacts its price."

Ian found he could not look into his eyes. Joshua floated before him, that distant enigmatic smile still on his face.

"Of all the places I have visited or shall visit, this is the one I shall come back to," Ian said.

Joshua nodded.

"You have gazed at man-made eternity," Joshua replied. "And Ian Lacklin the historian only wishes to visit so that he can look into the past."

Ian did not reply, for what Joshua said was true. If this was the potential of living across the millennium, then he would indeed prefer death. And in that thought Ian Lacklin started to discover something else, as well. All his life he had been a coward. In fact, at times he felt rather proud of his cowardliness and viewed it simply as the proper reaction of any intellectual. But he saw a deeper fear haunting Joshua. A fear of death so all-consuming that life in a mausoleum was thought by him to be preferable. Ian felt that he would never again fear death in quite the same way, having seen what the extreme could bring.

Joshua seemed bowed down, as if the weight of ages was oppressing him. And with that weight had come the loss of all vitality, all life—so that he was nothing but a husk, floating through the motions of living.

"I'll be back, Joshua, and we can spend long days talking, talking of all that you once saw."

"All that I once saw," Joshua said as if echoing his words.

"I've loaded our ship's memory right to capacity with your records, thank you for helping me with that. I know Richard will be fascinated with your medical data, and I can't begin to tell you how your early data library will help my research. Thank you again."

"You're welcome," Joshua replied, his voice barely audible. He seemed to be staring off into the distance, as if looking beyond to something Ian knew he could not see.

"I might not be awake when you return, Ian Lacklin. Just our talking for the last ten days has conjured up so many memories better left undisturbed. And each memory is a weight, a heavy chain dragging me down into a swirling circle of despair that I cannot escape. I may not be awake then when you return, and if not, come and visit me in the corridor of sleep and say hello, Ian Lacklin. Say hello to one who shall outlive you into eternity."

CHAPTER 8

Looking at the aft viewscreen, he could still see Joshua's unit, a small sphere of light suspended in the crosshairs of the high-magnification scanner. Ian finally turned his gaze away from the screen and looked over to Richard and smiled.

"Are we going to float out here forever?" Richard asked quietly, while offering a flask of gin. Ian nodded his approval and the flask floated across to his outstretched hand. Just as he started to take a pull on the straw, the doorway slid open and Ellen drifted through the hatch into the storage compartment that all knew was Ian's secret hiding place.

"So much for my *sanctum sanctorum*," Ian muttered.

Ellen settled down by his side and extended her hand to the flask.

"Good gods"—Richard gasped—"is this a sign that our beloved group psychologist is cracking up, running amok, and all that?"

"Shut up," she muttered in reply.

"And so touchy! Truly this is too much."

"Look, Croce, I knew Ian was in here trying to decide, and I thought I'd join him."

"Well, what do you think I should do?" Ian asked.

"I feel the same way you do," Ellen replied. "I'm torn. Our ship's memory banks are filled to capacity. I've got enough forms filled out to last me through half a dozen publications, and most of all I'm just sick. Especially after that one." She gestured toward the screen.

"But?" Richard interjected sarcastically.

"Yeah, but," Ellen replied. "That's just it, Ian, we're all being drawn by that one big *but*. A bit of mystery has been set, and I'd like to get a look at what this Dr. Franklin Smith set in motion. I must say that the videos of him are quite compelling."

Ian smiled weakly at her. They had watched the 1100-year-old tape made by Joshua's onboard security system. It was badly damaged but computer enhancement had restored many of the details. Smith had been powerful—his charismatic energy rippling across the millennium. His ebony features had carried a sense of great intellect paired with a ruthless drive for survival. Yes, the romantic image from the past had held Ian in its sway as well.

"He's long dead," Ian replied. "And if the odds are correct, chances are all his people are dead, as well. Their ship was an exile unit, and overcrowded far beyond its bearing capacity. True, he was a charismatic leader, one of the moving forces for the Great Outward Leap, but for his particular unit the odds were near impossible. I think this *Alpha/Omega* is just another unit."

"But curiosity, the bane of any good historian, haunts you, doesn't it?" Ellen asked.

"All right, let's be logical," Ian replied. "First off, our ship's memory is packed to capacity. We wouldn't store another byte of data if we wanted to. We've been out over four months, and it will take nearly that long to return."

"If this crate holds up," a voice said over the PA loud-speaker.

"Ahh, yeah, thanks for the encouraging reminder, Stasz." Ian looked up at the forward viewscreen, which was suddenly filled with the image of their grinning pilot, who had obviously been indulging with Richard.

"I thought this little room was my private domain!" Ian shouted. "First Richard, then Ellen, now you listening in. So where the hell is Shelley?"

"Right here, Ian." And the doorway slid open so that she drifted in to join them. "I was listening in on the intercom. There's been an open channel out of your cub-byhole for months, but you never knew it."

Oh, great. Then they had heard his mutterings in pri-vate, when he thought he was hiding from the rest of them. He suddenly realized with a flush of embarrassment that Shelley and the rest must have heard some of the com-ments he had mumbled of late concerning Shelley, as well.

He looked up at her and the moment of eye contact was enough. She blushed and he quickly turned away, and the other three chuckled.

"Highly unethical, some of the things you've said to yourself," Ellen admonished.

"Let's get back to the subject," Ian interrupted, trying to regain control of the conversation. "As Stasz reminds us on every single jump, there is a probability of disaster built into the Alpha-class spacecraft. We've been lucky. One more successful jump and we could be home."

"Or one jump to Delta Sag, which is only seven light-years away," Shelley replied. "We could check out the vicinity, and *then* head for home. It will only add a month and a half to the journey."

Ian realized that they were merely voicing the argu-ment that he'd wrestled with all day. Joshua had shaken him up. He had never expected something quite so chill-ing. But he was curious, as well. He had never orbited another star. Not surprising—he'd hardly ever been off-

campus. They would in fact be the first survey vessel ever
to orbit the Delta Sag binary. And since a number of
colony vessels had headed in this direction, there was the
possibility that they might find something.

"Come on, Ian," Shelley said softly. "Let's do it."

Ellen gave him a nudge and offered the flask.

"But you're almost out of forms," Ian said jokingly.

"I'll improvise. Hell, Ian, you've made my career on
this journey. I never thought it possible that I'd ever profit
from knowing you."

"Say, Ian, when she gets rich and famous, we should
go to some conference and pass the word about what C.C.
means."

Ellen turned with a roundhouse punch, and Richard
jerked aside, just barely missed losing his teeth. As Richard ducked, Ian was able to observe the absurd effects
created by trying to punch someone in zero G.

It took Shelley several minutes to subdue Ellen and
pull her out of the room.

"Not nice, Richard," Ian said admonishingly.

"But it was fun."

Knowing that the intercom line was hot, Ian didn't
reply immediately. After thinking their situation over for
a few minutes, he said, "All right, Stasz, punch us up for
Delta Sag. But this time I think I'll stay back here with
the flask and ride it out."

And when the drive finally kicked in with a vision-
blurring jolt, Ian could barely tell if it was the gin or
distortion that caused him to black out.

When the detection alarm kicked in, Ian and Shelley
were hunched over the display board examining some of
the records from *Unit 287*. For two weeks they had spent
every waking moment checking out the video recordings
and the historical data stored aboard the vessel. Ian was
still in a state near shock over the library, where he had

discovered thousands of works believed to have been lost in the Holocaust War.

The names of authors whose works were till now unknown scrolled across the catalog display, and Ian muttered with frustration when he tried to decide which to examine first.

"Look at these," Ian had cried. "The discovery of just one of these books would have been worthy of note, and we've found thousands. It will revolutionize our understanding of pre-Holocaust literature."

Shelley hung over his shoulder and watched as the names and works flashed across the screen.

"Who was this Mailer?" she asked.

"Someone obscure, I've read that his works are nothing but worthless mutterings."

"Then if that's the case, with our memory filled to capacity, shouldn't we dump him? I mean, Richard, Stasz, and Ellen are all howling for memory space."

"Yeah, maybe you're right," Ian replied, and he pushed the *erase* button to make room for something of more value.

"What about this Akhmedov? I never heard of him either."

"Good heavens, girl, and you my grad-ass ahh, I mean assistant. I should have you go back and reread your texts." And it was at that moment that the alarm kicked in.

Stasz quickly hit the override and within minutes they had gathered forward to see what was to come.

"No beacon functioning on this one," Stasz reported to the assembled crew, "but it's the biggest I've ever seen. Her mass triggered the alarm. She's only about five hundred A.U. off our main course, heading for Delta Sag. Should we jump down and check it out?"

Ian looked around and shrugged his shoulders. "What the hell?" he murmured. And turning, he went back to the computer board aft to ride out the velocity shifts and the gut-popping downshift to sublight.

"So that explains the mass," Stasz said. "There're two of them riding together."

They were on final approach, and the confusing shape of what appeared to be a triple torus mated to a Bernal sphere had finally, at closer examination, resolved itself into two distinct and different vessels.

"Shelley, can you get a clear design printout of this?" Ian asked.

Shelley ran the radar imaging through the computer file, and after several minutes of cross-matching with their records, the probable design and ship's data finally came up on the screen.

"Ian?"

"Yes?"

"What the hell is Albania?"

"Albania?" He floated over to Shelley's side and peered over her shoulder. He noticed that there was a faint but pleasant scent to her hair, and for a second his thoughts were diverted.

"What is it?" Ellen asked, and as he looked across at her Ian realized that she had noticed his diversion and he felt somewhat flustered.

Albania? Faint memories were stirred of old maps of southeastern Europe. He wasn't sure, but he had a recollection that they were some crazy nationalist group out of the Balkans. A number of ethnic groups had founded colonies in that final decade before the Holocaust, as an attempt to preserve their culture if the war finally came. So this then must be an ethnic preservation unit. He chuckled softly at the image of the Albanians greeting him at the door wearing gawdy peasant garb and gyrating to bizarre folk music.

This might be amusing, Ian thought lightly. They must be harmless.

"Ian, I'm getting a printout on the second unit," Shelley said. "It appears to be another ethnic group, it's a Serbo-Croatian Nationalist Liberation Unit."

Serbo-Croatians? Hell, even he was stumped by that.

He looked across at Ellen. "Amaze me and tell me that you know Serbo-Croatian, or whatever it is they speak over there."

"I'd like to lie, but I never even heard of Serbo-Croatian."

Ian didn't answer. He'd let them think that he knew all about them. He took over the data board from Shelley and accessed into their own library and into the library from *287* to find an answer.

After a half hour of silent study, he came to his conclusions. "Stasz, how about firing up our drive and getting us the hell out of here."

"What do you mean?" Richard interjected. "Hell, we're only a thousand kilometers away and closing. Come on, Ian, let's check these ethnic guys out—it might be interesting."

"Look, I'm the historian and the project leader. Trust me. Those Albanians and Serbo-Croatians were neighbors back on Earth. In fact, if you go over to that region today, you'll still find them gleefully slicing each other's throats when the sun goes down. They were doing it for a thousand years before the Holocaust. Hell, those crazy bastards helped to trigger a world war. If ever there were two groups of people who enjoyed slaughtering each other, it would be those two. I bet that they searched through all the cosmos just to find each other out here, so they could dress up in their ethnic garb and go at it. So let's just leave them alone with their friendly folk customs."

"Come on, Ian, let's go in just a little closer." This time it was Stasz.

"You're playing with fire."

"And here I thought you were turning heroic on us.

Now the old Ian comes back out again," Shelley said jokingly.

"Okay, go ahead, you crazies. But if they can get aboard this ship, you better learn how to speak Serbo or Albanian, or whatever it is, damn fast."

From less than a kilometer away they slowly circled the two units. The two colonies were docked to each other by several long tubes. Stasz hailed the vessels on every possible frequency but received no response. However, both ships gave clear indications that their reactors were functioning at full power, and from the exterior mirrors Ian could see reflected images of the inside indicating lights and movement.

It was the half-dozen suitless bodies floating between the two ships that finally sobered Ian's companions. Suddenly a number of vessels emerged from the Serbo-Croatian ship, and then from the Albanian. Both squadrons started in their direction and Ian's arguments finally took effect.

"I think we better get out of here," Stasz muttered as he punched up the sublight drive and started to pull away from the colonies.

However, after several minutes it soon became clear that their pursuers were gaining on them.

"You see, I told you so," Ian said dejectedly. "You guys wanted to check them out when I told you not to, and now they're going to force us to attend whatever it is they do to each other over there."

"Maybe they're not hostile," Ellen said hopefully.

"Not hostile? Did you see those bodies that had been deep-spaced? That didn't look too civilized to me."

"They're closing in at point twenty-three kilometers per minute," Stasz interrupted. "I'm pushing her to the max now, but it will take me another half hour to plot out our jump and go through purging and adjustment."

"Can't you speed it up?"

"You want to up our chance of disintegration from 1.4 to 20.2 percent?"

"Might not make a difference," Ian replied.

"Say, take a look at that!" Shelley cried, pointing at the aft screen.

A flash had emerged from the lead Albanian pursuit vessel.

"Looks like a primitive rocket," Stasz yelled. "If it's aimed at us, we're dead meat."

The rocket accelerated and within seconds its course was obvious, as it closed on the lead ship in the Serbo-Croatian pursuit squadron. In a noiseless flash of light the Serbo-Croatian craft disintegrated. The other vessels suddenly turned in their pursuit paths, accelerating away at right angles from their original trajectories. Rotating on their axes, they started to fire back.

"Good old rivalry saves our butts," Richard murmured. "Hate each other too much to let the other one get the prize."

More vessels soon emerged from the two colony ships and a major battle was underway. In the confusion the *Discovery* was soon forgotten, as each side prevented the other from closing in.

"Say, Stasz," Richard asked imploringly, "would you punch us out of here asap?"

Stasz chuckled and recited again the odds of disintegration with the jump. But the routine somehow did not have the same effect anymore.

"Albania," Ian repeated, shaking his head, bumming a flask from Richard. He headed aft to hide out when the shift hit.

Ian sat alone in the command bay as the others slept, and for a brief moment he was able to enjoy the total solitude that being the only one awake could bring. After nearly five months of voyaging together, each had learned the patterns of behavior that would generate the least amount of friction. Ian found that reversing his circadian cycle gave him the chance to quietly hide in his work when most of the others were asleep. As the *Discovery* soared across the vastness of empty space, Ian would spend hours in Stasz's couch contemplating the Doppler-distorted images or prowling through the vast accumulation of data stored in the ship's memory. And Ian finally realized that he was actually happy. In spite of the fears that still haunted him, he was enjoying himself, perhaps for the first time in his life.

First of all the vast and varied responsibilities of Earth were gone. All concern about rent, budgets, department meetings, and reviews by the Chancellor had vanished. Ian actually felt healthier, and he had to confess that Ellen's food, even when spiced with her occasional vitriolic tirades, was far better than his bachelor monstrosities. There was something far deeper, as well. For the first time in his life he felt as if he were doing something important, not just dreaming about the lives of others long dead. The sense of accomplishment was almost worth the bouts of terror that still assailed him. He found that he was actually learning to manage the nagging self-doubts when he had to make a decision that could be crucial to his survival, let alone the survival of others.

One self-generated disturbance, however, did give him pause for concern. He was experiencing an increasing number of fantasies about Shelley. She had somehow changed. When they had departed, she was still the kid who was playing at being the grownup housekeeper and guardian for a beloved uncle or older neighbor. Ever since the burning he had received from the Governor's daughter, Ian had sworn off females in general and young ones in particular. As a college professor he mainly associated with kids twenty years his junior, and he had learned long ago that they were a quick and easy way to a tribunal hearing on a morals charge.

But five months of close proximity was getting a little

too much to deal with. He knew that Stasz had absolutely no interest in Ellen's designs but was turning his attention toward Shelley, as well. But the few grab passes offered by the pilot had all resulted in cracked knuckles. So that possibility was out.

At times he thought Shelley was making a direct pass at him, and then again there were times when she seemed just a slightly gawky grad assistant who was trying to be helpful. But more and more of late, he found himself contemplating the tight slacks that Shelley had taken to wearing, and the press of her body against his when they were hovered over the computer display...

"Mind if I join you?"

Ian awoke from his reverie to find Ellen standing in the doorway. "Ahh, sure. Thought you'd be asleep."

"Felt like taking a midnight stroll." She chuckled softly. Coming forward, she slipped into the Co seat next to Ian.

"You look rather pensive."

"Oh, just watching the show pass by."

"It's rather frightening at times," Ellen said softly.

"How so?"

"Come on, Ian. In my book, you were the original coward. I thought you would still be quaking at the prospects of this voyage."

He didn't take offense at her statement. And rather than ducking it, he had a strange compulsion to talk it out. "First of all, I did feel terror, cold stark terror, when I finally started to realize what this voyage was. I can almost understand how medieval man was stunned and terrified by Copernicus. Before him the world was small, safe, the center of God's will. After Copernicus eternity stretched out before us and such a thing was beyond our ability to grasp, thus the blind terror of it all.

"When I realized just how far we would travel, just how far away from Earth we were going, how far we were traveling from that damn little campus, I was struck with fear. The thought of this frail, delicate body hurtling at jump speed for trillions of miles was beyond my ability to deal with on a rational basis. I tried to soothe myself with the thought of the romance of it, but that's a bunch of shit. There isn't any romance, there never is any romance when you're out doing it. Maybe years later we'll talk about how romantic it all was. The romance of adventure exists only in the memory. Any good historian could tell you that."

"Sounding philosophical tonight."

"Comes with soaring in space for too long. It gives you the chance, the time to separate yourself from the mundane. I think I can understand the attraction the explorers of long ago felt for the sea. Out *there* the mundane cares of the rest of the world were lost in a never-ending change which was the sea, the wind at your back . . ."

"But it's so cold," Ellen whispered. "I look out at this immensity and I feel so small, so alone."

"Precisely. And that is where you lose yourself. I've imagined at times that this voyage could soar on forever, across the endless sea."

"And I see it merely as a mission and then a trip home. Don't you want to go home, Ian?"

"What for? To go back to faculty meetings and the monthly confrontations with Dr. Ellen Redding?"

"All right, Ian, you made your point. You know, I've tried at times to analyze why we can't stand each other. For that matter, why I can't stand most people."

He was tempted to let fly with a sarcasm, but let it pass. Ellen was making an effort. Rare, to be sure, but it was an effort.

He took a deep breath and made the plunge. "When I hear the name Ellen Redding I picture a florid, freckled, five-foot-three, slightly overweight, middle-aging adolescent, who still behaves at times like she is the ingenue of the high school set."

He quickly held up his hand to ward off the explosion, but it didn't come. She just sat silently, and he wasn't sure if the blush on her face was a signal for a fireball or for tears.

"And I think she resents it all," Ian continued. "She wishes to be something else. The classic beauty, the truly talented artist, the person who lives in the same circle as the Chancellor or with the literati of New Bostem, and instead is stuck in a backwater town. So you lash out, Ellen. You lash out at this overweight, balding, none-too-competent history professor. A male of the species who can represent all the males who never gave you an even break just because of your sex and lack of sexuality. And I guess I'm saying this 'cause I'm a long way from home. I'm still a coward underneath it all, and I want to bury the hatchet."

"Ian, you never did learn tact. You never did learn how to tell the truth without cutting flesh."

She turned away for a moment. "I think I'd almost miss cutting you up."

"There's always Richard."

"That slob?"

"Sure he's a slob—a frustrated slob who never had the right connections in a system that required it. A slob who was a little too sensitive when it came to practicing medicine, and hid it with a couple of drinks too many. And anyhow, Ellen, you make him happy."

"I make him happy! I'm not sure I heard that correctly."

"Sure, Ellen, think of it. Where would you and Richard be if you didn't have each other to insult? I half believe we enjoy our antagonisms as much as we do our loves. It gives us the energy to face what otherwise would be a very boring existence. Think of it this way, Ellen, you make Richard happy in a deep personal way every time you insult him."

She turned and looked at Ian. She wasn't sure if his speech wasn't some sort of elaborate joke planned by

Richard and Ian, or if she was experiencing a moment of truth between the two of them.

Then the alarm kicked on and within seconds Stasz wandered sleepy-eyed, into the cabin to check the console printouts for navigation prompts.

As Ellen walked out of the cabin, Ian would have sworn that she smiled at him.

CHAPTER 9

Colonial Unit 122

First Completion Date: 2063

Primary Function: International Feminist Foundation. Organization founded by radical feminists in 1994 to "create a lifestyle totally removed from a male-dominated infrastructure."

Evacuation Date: According to Copernicus Base Record, July 19, 2083. Believed to be one of the first units to depart near-Earth space.

Overall Design: Single Torus 900 meters in diameter with central shaft 500 meters in length.

Propulsion: Standard Modification Design, strap-on matter/antimatter packs mounted to nonrotational central shaft.

Course: Delta Sag.

Political/Social Orientation: Anglo-American, Radical Feminist. Taught doctrine of removal of the male species. Thousands of sperm samples were taken and all

Y chromosome sperm destroyed. The result was billions of frozen X sperm, creating a potential "pool" capable of providing enough fertilization capabilities to last for several hundred generations.

"Hard Dock!" Stasz announced, turning to look back at the rest of the crew.

"Any reading yet on which unit this is?" Richard asked.

"There're no external markings," Shelley replied. "The beacon is off, and all I have to go on is the design. There are thirteen single-torus models listed in our records."

"Shall we go?" Ian said softly, as he eased out of his seat and drifted aft to the docking port. "Who's game for this one?"

"What the hell?" Richard responded as he slipped out and followed Ellen.

As they suited up with businesslike calm. Ian could remember the fear and anticipation of his first boarding, but that seemed like ages ago, as if he possessed the memories of someone else.

"We're throwing the hatch," Ian said as the manual airlock to the colonial unit slowly opened. Instinctively he braced himself as the hatchcover parted. A quick flash of memory caused his pulse to jump. But nothing was there except for the usual corridor leading to the second airlock.

They closed the doorway behind them, and in the soft glow of their headlamps Ian pulled the manual release for the inner airlock door.

"Holy shit!" Richard murmured. The words flowed out of him in reverent awe, as if he had suddenly looked into a celestial radiance.

The words were on Ian's lips, as well. A single woman stood before them, as if Eve had appeared incarnate from the Garden, her body clothed as was Eve's before the fall from grace.

"Damn me," Richard said, "what the hell do we have

these things on for? She looks safe enough without 'em."
And before Ian could stop him, Richard unsnapped his
helmet and pulled it off. He moved closer to the woman
and smiled, hoping the slight odor of gin would not prove
too offensive.

Her deep-blue eyes had a cold clearness that seemed
to mask a longing desire, her curly blond hair tumbled
down past her shoulders to just barely cover the full swell
of her breasts. She stood before him naked and inviting.

"Ahh, my child, do you understand what I'm saying?"

She nodded and smiled.

"My name is Dr. Croce. Ahh, well now, you see, being
of the medical profession my training requires that I must
inquire into your obvious state of excellent health. Do
you understand me?"

She nodded again.

"Good, my ahh... dear." He moved forward and
touched her lightly on the shoulder. "Would you mind if
I perhaps examined you a little more closely?..."

"Richard, you pig!" Ellen pushed forward to stand between the girl and the medico.

"Ahh, yes, I've heard of that word, 'pig'." The voice
was cold and chilling. Ian turned and found himself looking into a set of cold dark eyes. He stepped back as half
a dozen women floated out from a side corridor. They
were dressed like their comrade, but the business ends
of six antique pistols were enough to convince him that
he shouldn't ask questions about their choices in fashion.

"You see, sisters," the cold-voiced woman said, "it's
as we've learned. His first thought was that of exploitation."

"I can explain..." To those unfamiliar with him, Richard's voice sounded solemn and professional, but Ian could
detect the fear in it.

"Ah, now the pig will explain. That's always the case."

"You were right, Diana," the blond woman replied,
"the trap was almost too simple."

"Say, Ian, what the hell is going on over there?"

"Secure the airlock against entry, Stasz!" Ian shouted, but before he could say another word the cold-eyed woman held a small box against his neck. A numbing shock knocked him over. He was still conscious, but incapable of moving.

"Thank you, sister, I've been waiting for this liberation ever since I was assigned to these men. Please let me knock the other one down."

Ian recognized the last speaker as Ellen! Well, of all the gratitude, he thought sadly as two women hauled him away. At least, he thought philosophically, I'm still conscious and capable of enjoying the view.

"How long do you think it's been?" Ian asked.

"Don't know—a day, maybe a day and a half," Richard replied wearily. "Their time measurement is radically different from ours, so it's hard to tell."

"I wish they'd give my clothes back." Ian felt ridiculous sitting naked in a bare cubicle alongside the equally overweight and equally naked doctor.

Richard started to chuckle.

"Damn it, I don't see anything funny! What the hell are you laughing at?"

"I never thought the two of us would be paraded before ten thousand naked women and extolled as examples of manhood. Think of it, Ian, ten thousand women seeing a man for the first time, and it had to be us. Imagine what fantasies they'll have about us afterward."

"Fantasies my bare ass," Ian grumbled as a key clicked in the door. It was time for another examination session.

"Sisters, our two specimens here are evidence of just how degenerate the male of the species truly is. Thank our grandsisters for liberating us from *that*." Diana pointed with contempt at Ian and Richard. Murmurs of agreement arose from the several hundred women gathered in the lecture hall to attend what Diana said would be an "interactive examination of the subspecies male."

As Diana gazed at him in contempt, Richard tried a weak smile. Ian scanned the audience and found to his amazement that after several days of seeing naked female flesh in every form and shape, the initial excitement was wearing thin. Oh, to be sure, an occasional woman caught his eye, but given his current situation, tied and spread-eagled on an examination table, he felt it best not to let his gaze linger on any particular attraction.

But he did notice Ellen and Shelley sitting in the front row and made eye contact with both of them. Taking a closer look at Ellen, he almost started to laugh as she positioned her body in a desperate attempt to cover all areas of interest. But Shelley was another story. She sat back in what could only be considered an attempt at display and regarded him with a cool look of playful invitation. In desperation he quickly looked away. Good lord, that woman was torturing him!

"Sisters," Diana said, interrupting his thoughts, "we've had our opportunity to examine these creatures both physically and mentally. Now, in yet another demonstration of our liberated society, I think it is only correct that we allow them to show their own masculine weaknesses by giving them the opportunity to question us in turn.

"Go ahead, ask us anything," Diana said with scorn, "anything at all."

Ian and Richard were silent.

"Are you afraid, too?"

"Understand I am a doctor," Richard said, attempting to sound authoritative, "so this is only a question out of my professional curiosity."

"Go on, *Doctor*," Diana hissed. "We already saw a display of your professional interest in Sister Carrie." She nodded toward the willowy blonde from their first encounter.

"All right then. As I understand it, you are a feminist group that holds all men in contempt."

"Correct, and in fact the only logical thing any normal woman would do."

"Second, in the thousand years since you've left Earth you've used only X-chromosome sperm to create more women."

"As is only proper, you see, Doctor. With our huge bank of edited sperm we've eliminated the need for men and for that—how shall I say?—*function* you once provided."

"I see." Richard was trying to look professional, and Ian almost found himself laughing at the naked doctor trying to stare down his disdainful audience.

"Then what do you do for, ah, recreation?"

"Do you mean sexual gratification, Doctor?"

"Yes. I mean, after all, ladies, without any men around..." And his voice trailed off.

Angry mutterings could be heard in the crowd.

"Why doctor, I'll satisfy your disgusting prurient interest, which we realize all men naturally harbor. Doctor, we simply find our necessary gratification in each other."

"Good lord, I've died and gone to heaven," Richard muttered.

"What was that?"

"Nothing, nothing at all."

"Now, I'm a healthy man, not past my prime," Richard said in reply. "Don't you think some of you ladies—say you, Carrie, or even you, Diana—aren't you curious just to see what it might be like with a man?"

The audience chamber exploded in outraged shouts of disgust. A torrent of abuse showered down on the two, so that for some minutes Ian feared that they were about to be lynched by a thoroughly incensed mob.

"Keep your damn mouth shut," Ian hissed, "or so help me..."

"So help you, what?"

"I don't know, but so help me something."

Suddenly Ellen was up and pointing at Richard. "That's what I've had to put up with," she shouted. "It's still that way back on Earth! Thank you, oh, thank you for saving me." She started to cry, and Carrie hurried to embrace her.

"Traitor!" Richard shouted. "You didn't act exploited when you were trying to get into Stasz's pants."

Outraged howls roared over the crowd as, sobbing hysterically, Ellen was escorted from the room by Carrie.

"Just shut up, Richard," Ian begged, "otherwise I'll strangle you the first chance I get."

"See, sisters, see the natural aggressiveness coming out, even between two so-called friends."

The two prisoners fell silent, and eventually the outraged women calmed down.

"You, Lacklin," Diana asked, "do you have any questions?"

In spite of his sense of absurdity, Ian couldn't help but approach the situation as an historian. He felt that he might even have been participating in a historical first—the first interview by a historian in deep space while naked in front of three hundred naked women.

"Just a minor question first. Why no clothes?"

"Why not?" Diana replied. "Clothing was exploitive and designed by men to enslave us. Here we are sisters, and free of such things. And besides, the climate is completely controlled."

"Do you understand your historical roots?"

"Oh, quite well. Our memory systems have survived intact, and our leaders, who first created our society a thousand years ago, live yet in those memories. Through their inspired guidance we re-learn daily of our ansisters' exploitation by your gender. Each generation that is born here learns it as well from our teaching library."

That would explain their almost perfectly preserved twenty-first-century pre-Holocaust speech, Ian suddenly realized. The vocabulary and pronunciation would be learned from an unchanging source, thereby guiding the language and arresting it at a particular point. A philologist would be fascinated with their society—it's a living example of a language long altered on Earth.

It was fascinating, as well, since the founding philosophy had survived, unlike the Friends of the Light who had quickly evolved into something beyond the wildest imaginings of their founders.

"So you artificially inseminate out of your frozen bank and then train your children through the library."

"Not artificially" came a voice from the audience. "Ours is the natural way; yours the abomination."

"Have you ever tried it?" Richard shouted back. "It's not so bad."

"God damn it, Richard," Ian shouted before the uproar swept over them, "are you trying to get us killed?"

"We'd prefer if you didn't take Her name in vain," Diana said coldly. "And as for getting killed, you might not be too far off the mark."

Richard looked at Diana with a weak smile. "May I ask one or two other questions?"

Diana nodded an affirmative.

"How do you administer your system?" Ian said before Richard could ask another question.

"We have a system of support groups."

"I'm sorry, I'm not familiar with that term. What is a support group?"

Several of the women laughed.

"We are all organized into groups of ten sisters who provide support and encouragement to each other. From each such group one is selected who, with nine others selected by their groups, participates in the next level of administration. So the structure progresses up to the Sister Eldest, the position I now hold."

"It sounds like a logical management system," Ian replied, trying to smile in a friendly fashion.

"Watch it, sisters," Diana said sarcastically, "he's appearing to support us, but we all know that underneath he still wishes to exploit."

"Okay." He hesitated for a second, unsure if "okay" signaled agreement or expression of anger. They didn't show any stronger hostility so he assumed his colloquialism had been correct.

He tried for another. "I can relate to that and to your struggle."

"Don't patronize us!" several dozen shouted.

He wasn't sure of that term either, but the tone of the response was enough. "Let me make this a more personal question then. It's obvious you don't like us, I can accept that. So why not return our clothes and Richard and I will be on our way. And if our two sisters desire, they can head out, as well. Is that okay?"

Diana's eyes narrowed suspiciously. "Why? So you can run back to your male-dominated world and give them the word as to where we are?"

Diana turned away from Ian and faced the audience. "Sister Ellen has already told me that you can make a voyage of a thousand years in just a matter of months. No thank you. We don't want you running home and then bringing back your contemptible breed to gawk and exploit. We know a pig named Stasz is hiding in your ship. Sisters, once we figure out the way, we'll break into the pigs' ship and take it for ourselves!"

The women cheered while Ian looked at Richard and grimaced. The women were serious, and there would be no turning on the charm and talking their way out. Ian looked appealingly at Shelley, hoping that she would speak out. She looked him straight in the eye then brushed her hair back off her small rounded breasts, so that he could see them more clearly. She favored him with a tiny smirk.

"So, what are you going to do with us?"

Diana smiled at his question.

"The Primary Council support group has debated that question and we've come up with a proper answer.

"Our frozen sperm is a thousand years old, and increasing numbers of samples are flawed after the extended deep freeze. Sister Ellen has assured me that your medical backgrounds are adequate, even if your physical appearance is substandard.

"Therefore," Diana continued, "we propose to use you to resupply our bank."

"Suppose we won't cooperate," Ian snapped back, his dignity insulted by the mere thought of what she was suggesting.

"We've thought of that, as well. We understand that you men find the watching of the sexual act between women to be particularly exciting. Perhaps after several such voyeuristic experiences you'll be willing to, how shall I say, give us a hand."

"Oh, God, I've died and gone to heaven," Richard moaned.

The doorway slipped open and Shelley signaled them to be silent. Ian had half suspected it all along, but knowing it was true caused him to kiss her with relief.

"Let's go," Shelley whispered. Ian nudged Richard awake. Richard looked at him bleary-eyed and groaned. He had been taken out hours before for a "session," or at least that's what Diana had said, and must have been returned when Ian was already asleep.

Ian pointed to the door where Ellen and Shelley stood.

"Is this an escape?" Richard asked. "Well, if so, count me out, you'll never make it."

"Come on, asshole," Ellen commanded, "we're going."

"Leave without me, this setup isn't so bad. At least let me offer a couple more samples first."

Ellen slipped into the room and pulled out a stun prod like the one Diana used. "If you don't get your ass up and moving," Ellen hissed, "I'm going to put it on your butt and jolt your backside clear across this room. Now move!"

"All right, damn it." Richard cursed wearily and got to his feet. Ellen fell in behind him and Shelley led the way. Twice they encountered a "sister," and in both cases Shelley managed to drop them with a stunner. And in both cases Richard had to be dragged away from his attempt to "make sure there was no lasting damage."

Finally they reached the airlock entry and a brief scuffle ensued as they fought their way past half a dozen guards then finally managed to secure themselves inside the airlock.

"Now let's hope Stasz didn't decide to abandon us here," Ian said.

"Not to worry," Ellen replied. "I managed to lift the radio out of my suit and I stayed in touch with him." She pulled the unit out of the pouch hanging from her shoulder, which was the only stitch of clothing she had on.

"We're in the airlock, Stasz."

"How the hell do I know it's you?" The fear in his voice was obvious.

"Listen, you drunken idiot," Richard replied, "I know you've already snatched two of my bottles and hidden them under your bunk since we left Earth. God knows how many more you've taken while I've been away. In fact, that's the only damn reason I've come back—"

The airlock hatch opened.

"Blast my eyes with a nova," Stasz muttered as Ellen and Shelley drifted past. Shelley even stopped for a moment, leaned up and kissed Stasz on the cheek, then pushed off and floated away to the main cabin—the three men looking after her.

"What happened?" Stasz asked, as he looked mockingly at his two now slightly self-conscious companions.

"Paradise," Richard replied.

"Docking unlatched," Shelley said, her eyes on the main instrument board. She was back in a light coverall, and Ian found himself looking at her and imagining what he had seen earlier.

There was a faint tug of gravity as the maneuvering thrusters turned them out and away from the torus.

"My compliments, Ellen," Ian said softly.

She looked back at him and smiled. "It was Shelley, as well. She had come across a description of the unit in the library banks some weeks back. She pointed it out to me and we both had a good laugh wondering what it would be like if we ever came across them. The moment I saw Carrie I knew what we had hit into, and realized that I had to play along and wait for a chance to escape."

"Just how far did you play along?" Stasz asked leeringly. "Yeah, the doc told me about what them girls did to each other back there."

Ellen fell strangely silent.

"You seemed to enjoy yourself," Richard said, directing his comment to Shelley. "I swear you loved every minute of teasing poor old Ian and me."

She smiled knowingly and without comment looked back to the board.

"Did they torture you at all?" Stasz asked, already imagining all sorts of exquisite possibilities.

"Ahh, what torture," Richard said softly.

"Just think about this for torture," Ellen said suddenly, with a malicious gleam in her eye. "I was thinking of letting it ride for another couple of days, but then I found out what they had planned for you two so I took the extra risk and tried the breakout at once. It seems they found the old way of taking sperm samples to be rather repugnant. So, my dear doctor, their medical people came up with a suggestion that Diana approved of right after they had their first specimen-gathering session for you."

"Oh, I can just imagine what delights they had planned," Richard said smoothly, "though to beat that first session would have been darn near impossible. Ian, my old comrade, you should have been there to see it. Why, it was a true delight. You really missed something while you were asleep. And then these damn women here came and dragged us away before you had a chance."

Ian gave the two girls a look of reproach.

"You could have let me have one session," Ian replied, "before liberating us."

"Maybe we should have, you ungrateful slug," Ellen responded, her face aglow with a malevolent smile, "but my dear sister Shelley talked me out of waiting. You see, my fine chauvinistic friends, the medical team suggested to Diana that a simple operation could cut off the part of your body that they needed; it could have been rigged to a bio support unit to produce all the sperm they'd ever need. They just did that little show for you to get a sample, so they could check out if you were viable and worth the effort.

"If the operation had worked, they planned the same for you, my dear Ian."

Not another word was said as the three men went aft to drink.

CHAPTER 10

Colonial Unit 13

First Completion Date: 2023

Primary Function: Cosmos Society. Organization of pro-space activists. One of the first units to demonstrate the feasibility of the O'Neill Cylinder design.

Overall Design: Single cylinder, 1400 meters by 350 meters.

Propulsion: Matter/Antimatter.

Course: SETI Anomaly One. Galactic Core.

Political/Social Orientation: Multinational Japanese, Russian, English. Cited by Beaulieu as "a colonial unit of exceptional promise, showing the possibilities of international harmony through peaceful cooperation in space." With the coming of the Holocaust the citizens of *13* voted to evacuate rather than be turned against each other by their less-civilized ancestors below.

"Jesus, what the hell is this!"

The jump-down from light speed was complete, but Ian was ignoring Stasz's shouted questions because he was still nauseated from the transition.

"Get on the board, Ian."

Convinced for the moment that dinner wasn't going to come rushing back up, Ian pushed forward to hover behind Stasz's shoulder.

"I'm getting a lot of debris," Shelley called from the Co's position. "I've locked onto a beacon two thousand klicks ahead, declination five degrees off. But there are no significant mass readings."

"Ian, look at this!" Shelley dialed the CRT up to a higher magnification.

A human body was at screen-center slowly tumbling through space.

"I'm picking up more, Ian, dozens of them. Do you want to look?"

He shook his head and turned away.

Within minutes Stasz was maneuvering the *Discovery* through a nightmarish jumble of debris—the twisted remnants of what had once been a vessel of several hundred thousand tons. On a number of occasions hard maneuvering was required to avoid torn hunks of metal and, in one case, a mummified fragment that had once been human.

"As near as I can estimate," Stasz reported, "a thin cloud of debris is traveling outward from Delta Sag at a velocity of just over 230 miles per second."

Delta Sag was straight ahead of them and outshining all the other stars in the heavens. Another half hour's run would have jumped them within twenty A.U. of the star. But the signal beacon had caused them to stop and jump down into a floating funeral.

Ian scanned the trajectory backplot and passed it over to Stasz.

Stasz punched in the data and within seconds had a

response. "Approximately fifty-two years, six months outward bound from Delta Sag," Stasz reported, "assuming constant velocity."

"I have the beacon source on visual," Shelley announced.

The five of them huddled around the primary screen as the image came up. It was a nondescript hulk of interstellar flotsam slowly tumbling end over end.

"Approximately a hundred meters long by fifty wide," Stasz reported. "It looks like the reactor core. It's still hot, I'm picking up some trace readings."

Even as Stasz spoke, the *Discovery* lurched slightly as it weaved past a large fragment that its shields could not vaporize. Stasz guided the vessel back onto an intercept course and before the hour was over he was fine-tuning the final approach that would bring them up alongside the reactor unit.

"This is a waste, Ian," Ellen said, "whatever colony unit this was, it's been blasted beyond recognition."

The others murmured their agreement. They were flying formation with a drifting junk-yard—torn metal, shredded shielding, shards of glass, and mummified bodies.

"I need to find out more," Ian replied coldly. "We started out aimless, but with each step farther out, the path seemed to point us into this direction, and to that star." He pointed at Delta. "Now, damn it, we're only a fraction of a light-year out from it and we find this. I've got to know why. Was this an accident or was it something else?"

"You mean Smith's colony?" Richard asked.

"Isn't it obvious?"

"By my hairy butt," Stasz shouted. "There's someone aboard that hulk!"

They crowded forward to see where he was pointing.

"There, in that window, I saw a light flashing. Look, it will roll into view again in another couple of seconds. *There*, there it is!"

As the window came into view, a strobe flashed once,

then again and again in rapid succession, and in the flashing light Ian thought he saw a figure waving.

After half a dozen passes they were convinced that there was somebody alive in there. But how to get at him?

Twelve hours later they were still debating the question.

"Look," Stasz repeated yet again, as if they were ignorant children. "First, there's no docking port."

"But there does seem to be an airlock."

"We're not sure its functional," Stasz replied. "Second, there's only one person in here who's had experience with an EVA propulsion device, and that's me. And if you think I'm going out into that floating junkyard, you're crazy. Remember, comrades, if I buy it, who the hell is going to fly you back home?"

None of them liked to be reminded of that. Stasz was all they had, and as such, he was treated with special care when it came to dockings and explorations.

"So, who wants to go?" Shelley asked again, and all were silent.

"We could always tie a tether line to someone, he could push out, and if he runs into a problem we could reel him back in."

"Well, sister," Richard said reproachfully, "what do you mean 'him'? I thought after that dose of liberation at our last visit, you would be more than eager to prove yourself yet again."

"Just remember, buster, it was I who saved you from an operation that might have improved your personality."

"And you never did tell us, sister Ellen, just how sisterly you and Carrie got. My, my, I would have loved to have seen that show."

"You rotten son of a bitch!" Ellen stood up with such vigor that she tumbled from her seat and catapulted clear into the forward cabin.

Her shrieks filled the air and it was some seconds before the rest of them realized that the shrieks were not screams of rage but of terror.

They pushed forward and Ian felt his heart skip over into a near palpitation as he looked toward the forward window. A mummified face was looking in the window from the outside. But this mummy was grinning and its eyes were rolling. It brought up a space-suited hand and waved.

"Guess that settles the question of whether we go to the neighbors or the neighbors come here," Richard said. "I better get a bottle, it looks like he needs a drink."

"Crack one for me, as well," Ellen said hoarsely. "I need it."

"Elijah, they called me Elijah Crump." He spoke slowly, each word formed distinctly and with effort, as if every syllable was a physical form that had to be worked over before expelled.

With quiet ceremony Richard drifted forward and offered a drink container, but first he shook it lightly. The tinkle of ice could be heard.

"Richard, should you?" Ellen asked.

Elijah looked at him, a glint of suspicion in his eyes.

"Are you from Sagit?"

"Sagit?" Ian asked.

"He must mean Delta Sagittarius," Shelley interjected, and pointed back to the front of the ship where the one star now dominated the sky before them.

"Yes, Delta Sagittarius." He stumbled over Sagittarius but they knew what he had said. "Curious name, what does it mean? We never did know."

Ian wrestled with so many questions. He had almost leaped upon Elijah the moment he had cleared the airlock, so eager was he to find out why. Why? There were so many whys, but he had to be patient. Elijah was not the typical image of what one expected to come floating in for a friendly visit.

First off, his suit was downright dangerous. It was of an ancient pattern, last seen in Earth environment a millennium ago. Patched and repatched in a crazy-quilt pattern that looked like the efforts of a hallucinating seamstress. He was clothed in a set of coveralls that had been worked on in the same way, worn and threadbare from a thousand cleanings, matching the appearance of the man who wore them.

Elijah was lean, gaunt, and stretched out thin, his fingers long and sensitive, his high forehead fringed with a thin wisp of snow-white hair that matched the long flowing beard framing his face. Eagerly his eyes darted from one to the other of them, drinking in the sight of them; yet his look was also one of suspicion and fear.

"I haven't spoken to anyone in, how long is it?..." He lapsed into silence again, then noticed the drink still being offered by Richard.

Tentatively he took the container in his hand and brought the straw to his lips.

Tears came to his eyes.

"Bless you," he whispered. "I remember now, it's... it's called alcohol."

"Gin, my man," Richard replied cheerfully, "and the best to be had in this part of the cosmos."

"You were saying that you hadn't spoken to anyone," Ian interjected, fearful that Richard would start in on a comparative study of alcohol that would drag their guest into a numbing oblivion. "How long has it been?"

Elijah nodded his head slowly, took another sip and savored it.

"I remember a name for it, we called it godt. I had a chronometer aboard, back there." He gestured vaguely back toward the airlock. "It broke after measuring fifty-one godt."

"That's Old Russian for years," Ian whispered in quiet amazement.

Elijah took another sip and smiled gravely at them. "I

have survived upon that hulk alone. The other survivors died within the first year, and I was left alone. Alone after the destruction. It's been at least fifty years," he whispered, "since I have talked to another man."

Elijah started to laugh.

> "Alone, alone, all, all alone,
> Alone on a wide, wide sea!
> And never a saint took pity on
> My soul in agony."

Ian sat enrapt, but it was Shelley who interrupted.

"I've heard a fragment of that."

"Coleridge, *The Ancient Mariner.*"

"We've only a fragment," she continued. "The rest is believed lost."

"I know it all, right in here," Elijah said, pointing to his head. His voice rose up with a deep sonorous tone that echoed through the ship.

> "I closed my lids, and kept them close,
> And the balls like pulses beat;
> For the sky and the sea, and the sea, and the sky
> Lay like a load on my weary eye,
> And the dead were at my feet."

He stopped and looked at them.

"I'm sorry, I was alone, you see. Never a voice to respond, never a soul to listen as I shouted my words to the universe."

Ian could hardly respond, stunned by the magnitude of what he was observing. Fifty years alone, lost in the endless reaches of the universe! "What happened?" he asked tentatively.

Elijah took another sip and there was a wild glint in his eye.

"'For I alone have lived to tell thee this tale!'"

"What?"

"You don't realize, my friends, that I've waited two score and ten years to utter those simple words, 'for I alone have lived to tell thee this tale,' can't you see? Can't you see what this means?" His voice broke and he started to sob.

Ian looked across at Richard and the others.

"Not now, Ian, don't push him yet. It can wait," Richard said softly. "It can wait, let him have his drink."

Richard gently took Elijah by the arm and led him astern.

"A nation, no, a race," he shouted, "and down from across the millennium I am all that is left of my world, for I am Lazarus returned from the realm of the dead to tell thee all!"

"I was working in the backup reactor housing when they hit us." Ian turned with a start of fear. It was his watch, and as the others slept he had settled back to watch Elijah's slowly tumbling realm and the sharp, cold light of Delta Sag. He had never heard Elijah's quiet approach.

Ian beckoned for Elijah to join him in the Co's chair. He was no longer wearing the bizarrely patched coveralls, and he was freshly shaved and washed. Elijah looked at Ian and smiled softly. Ian was shocked to notice that most of his teeth were missing.

Elijah looked out the starboard window and stared at the slowly turning reactor unit.

"That was my entire world, nay, my entire universe. Main corridor eighty-three meters, fifty-two point one centimeters from main bulkhead to bulkhead. Shall I tell you how many tiles were set in the floor? How many were cracked and what each crack looked like? How about screws securing each air vent? I spent eternity floating, nameless, voiceless, eternally alone. Ah, such will be my eternity in Hell for having endlessly cursed the name of God in my madness."

Elijah looked back to Ian and smiled again. "I'm not mad, Ian Lacklin, not mad at all. Perhaps I am saner than any man alive, for I have learned the power of waiting, but I shall not make you wait. First I will tell you all, then you can tell me what I desire. Will you tell me of the paradise of my grandsires, where you walk upon the outside of your world and all is green and blue skies above? But first I will tell you."

Ian nodded and smiled encouragingly. He was half afraid that Elijah was tottering on the edge of a complete break-down, and when that came, his message would be lost forever.

"As I was saying, I was working on the backup reactor when they came."

"Who?"

"Ah, yes. From Delta Sagit, the followers of the Father."

"The Father?"

"Ah, yes, forgive me. You don't know. My world . . . I believe you call them colonies, had at last made Sun Fall. I was, let's see, sixteen that year, and already proven on the reactors and bio support."

Ian looked at him in amazement. Sun Fall he called it. A journey of a thousand years and at last they make Sun Fall. What it must have been like, arriving in a new realm.

"I can remember it. Our world was indeed desperate when we arrived. Across the millennium of the voyage some systems had failed, others had gradually been depleted, and we needed what our science people called a gas giant with hard-surfaced satellites, so that necessary resources could be mined. Coming in on Delta Sagit also gave us a new energy source, which we had already been exploiting through the use of parabolic mirrors.

"There are five gas giants around Delta Sagit and we

went into, how do you say—" He waved his hands vaguely in a circular motion.

"Orbit?" Ian prompted.

"Yes, orbit, that's the word, around the second farthest from the sun. Even as we arrived, they were waiting for us."

"Who? Was the Father's name Franklin Smith?" Ian ventured.

Elijah looked at him with incredulous eyes. "How did you know?"

"We've been following his path since the beginning."

"They said he was a great prophet," Elijah said, "who spoke of the Satan that had driven them into the Hegira.

"Our beacon was on as we approached. For five years before orbit we had intercepted some of their broadcasts, and they were aware of us, as well."

"Who are they?" Ian asked.

"They are followers of the Father," Elijah repeated in a vague singsong manner.

"You say they met you?"

"Remember, Ian Lacklin, I was not even of one score years. We of my age and station had no word of our leader's decisions, you see, our society was ruled by a philosophos."

"I don't recognize that . . ."

"From Plato, at least that's what I remember. I only saw the Father's delegation once, when they first docked with us. They were tall men and women, proud in their bearing, with dark faces and eyes that bespoke some inner vision. At least, that is how I remember, but you know the tricks that memory plays with an old man."

Ian nodded, trying to envision the encounter between two alien cultures separated by a thousand years from the common cradle of their birth.

"Our philosophos then told us that we were leaving. He said that they desired of us what we would not give and told us to do what we would refuse. Therefore, we would leave. We had but one month to stock up enough raw material for the replicator machines, and then we left."

"You had replicator machines?" Ian asked.

"Yes, a replicator. We always had them, don't you?"

Ian shook his head. "According to Beaulieu, they were only legend, machines that could be programmed to make whatever was desired, as long as enough raw material was fed in from the other end. Before the Holocaust some ninth-generation devices were used to mass-produce elements for the colonial development, but true replicators, capable of producing just about anything, including models of themselves, were only in the developmental stage when the war came. At least, so Beaulieu thought."

"Ah, so I see," Elijah said pityingly.

"What was it they wanted?"

"I don't know."

"You don't know?"

"Have you ever been sixteen and in love? Her name was Rachel..."

Ian nodded and understood. In the reality of sixteen-year-olds, there were some things even more important than the destiny of worlds.

"So we left. For six months we accelerated up and away, using the hydrogen mined from the gas giants along with matter/antimatter drives. And then there came the day."

His voice broke and he looked out the window at the ship.

"You know, she's over there still," Elijah said softly.

"Who?"

"My beloved Rachel. You realize I couldn't send her out with the rest. I found her a year or so after the dark day." He stopped for a minute, as if trying to control himself, and then pushed on. "I found her floating in the wreckage and brought her back. A room in my area had been ripped open to space. I tied my love in there with a cable, so she wouldn't float away. You know, I went to visit her every day and looked through the window at her. I said good-bye to her before coming. I asked her if she wanted to come with me but she said no, she wanted to stay with our world, forever sixteen. I said good-bye to her and she said good-bye to me and said she would miss me . . .

> "My love she sleeps,
> And may her sleep,
> As it is lasting so be deep,
> Soft may the worms about her creep."

His voice started to rise and crackle like old parchment being mishandled.

"It's all right, old boy." Ian turned with a start, and there was Richard smiling at the two of them, drink in hand. Ian sighed with relief.

"She understands, my good man, she understands," Richard said soothingly. "Here, have a little bracer." And he offered a chilled drink container.

Elijah snatched the container and took a long, deep pull.

"You were talking about the day," Ian asked softly. Richard gave him a look of reproach, but he decided to push ahead anyhow.

"I was working on the reactor, changing a fuel rod. Routine sort of thing. Suddenly it was as if my world had slammed into a solid rock. I thought we had taken a—what's the word?"

"Meteor . . . asteroid?"

"Yes, asteroid hit. I had heard of such things. We had a collision drill once a year. In fact, it was such a ritual that it was a festival day. The last one was the first time Rachel and I . . ." Elijah suddenly looked at them with cold clear eyes. "But that is gone forever."

His voice now took on a clipped urgency, as if he were

making some official report that had waited half a century to be given.

"The first salvo hit the torus in sections one through twenty. I went to the primary observation port and saw entire sections going up, exploding outward in flashes of light, tumbling debris, and shattered bodies. I saw it, I saw it! My God, that was my family, my mother and father! Damn you, damn you bastards forever!"

Richard placed a hand on his shoulder and Elijah looked at him with a haunted expression.

"Maybe you shouldn't," Richard said.

Elijah gave him a weak smile. "You know, I never saw them—I mean, who it was that did it. I saw the flash of the beams, but nothing else. I knew at once that somehow the followers of the Father had caught up with us. The beam weapons slashed out, again and again, with such neat surgical precision, slicing out section after section. The imbalance of the cylinder now started its own actions, ripping it apart from the central core that I was in.

"We screamed in impotent rage as the beam finally caught us out and slashed the core wide open.

"The section that I was in separated, cut from the main. 'Subreactor one and agro research and development section one, reporting in. Is there anyone there, is there anyone there?'"

He looked again at the hulk then turned back to them.

"Ten of us with air. We had thrown enough emergency locks to seal the section off. Six of them were badly injured, mostly from a radiation spill in the containment area.

"We fought for weeks. Patching leaks, stabilizing the research lab, and creating an environmental support system. We alone had survived. We found a couple of suits and rigged up an airlock, and thus started my scavenging operations. I would crawl through the corridors, pushing past the bodies. You know, a body can make excellent fertilizer. Oh, you'll do it if there's need enough. You know, you can do something else, as well. They're frozen dry, all you have to do is add a little water and the meat's almost as tasty as fresh," Elijah whispered.

Ian was unable to respond.

"The others couldn't stand it. I watched them go, one by one. They'd crawl into the airlock, some of them crying, others praying. One was laughing. They'd pop the door and take the leap. The Big Leap, that's what we called it. I'd watch them struggle out there, and later I'd go out after 'em. After all, they were fresh..."

Ian was stunned.

"There was nothing else you could have done," Richard said, his voice soft and soothing. "There was nothing else for you, it was necessary in order to survive."

Elijah looked at him and smiled. "Conservation, recycling, that was the world, the world of my forefathers. So I lived, I salvaged and lived, forever alone, in a world of floating death. Anyhow, it tasted quite good. Still does, you know."

He smiled at Richard. "If you want, I'll go out and get you one. I've got a whole stockpile of legs. Only the best for my friends."

"No, that's quite all right, quite all right, my friend," Richard replied, making a supreme effort not to show his emotions. Ian floated in the corner and tried not to gag.

"Rachel and I..." Elijah continued. "My poor, dear Rachel who floated in an airless room. And the one book, treasured in the museum. A book from before the Great Sailing. I found it floating in the wreckage. *Literature of the English-Speaking People*. Oh, I know it by heart, I do. I know it all by heart, for I read it to Rachel every day, and I shouted it to the heavens my entire life as I floated with my dinner in that corridor—eighty-two meters, fifty-two point one centimeters."

He looked over at the hulk again.

"'Let us fly these troubled waters, Ahab, let us come hard about.'"

He turned back to them with imploring eyes.

"'For I alone have lived to tell thee this tale.' Please, for God sake, take me away from here."

Elijah looked at Ian slyly and reached into his pocket.

"In payment Ian, in payment I'll give you this and yet another legend to pursue. But it's our secret." And so saying, he gave a paranoid look at Richard. "Only one, there's only one and I can't share."

Ian hesitated for a moment, fearful of some horror, but Richard came up to Ian's side and whispered.

"It's all right, it means he trusts you, if it's a piece of meat just pocket it, thank him, and leave. It's a bonding gift."

Richard smiled at Ian, nodded at Elijah, and floated out of the room, leaving the two of them alone. Ian smiled uncomfortably at Elijah and cleared his throat. If this is a piece of meat, Ian thought, I'll get sick, I know it, and he braced himself.

Elijah drew out his hand and opened it. A slender metal rod six inches long and the diameter of a straw floated up. A small blue button jutted from one end. The strange shimmer to the metal caught Ian's eye and he drew closer. It could have been a swizzle stick from Richard's drinking kit.

"What the hell?..."

"It scared the hell out of me," Elijah said softly.

"What?"

"The thing that owned that rod."

"What thing?" Ian suddenly noticed his heart was racing.

"The thing."

Ian gulped. "Do you mean an alien?"

He snatched the rod out of the air and nervously examined it. It was cool to the touch and a minuscule flowing script curled around the length of the shaft. He had never seen such writing before and with that realization his hands started to shake.

"How did you get this?"

"Promise you won't tell, the others might get mad at me, 'cause I didn't save any. You're the leader so I have to tell you but not the others." There was a pleading whine to his voice.

Ian nodded in agreement, not really paying attention to the words, as if he was listening to the fearful chatter of a little child.

"All right then." Elijah drew closer.

"It knocked on my door, it did. Honest, I heard a knock on the airlock. I looked out the window and there it was, a ship docked to mine. So I popped the door and, sweet holy of holies." His voice rose to a near shriek and Ian had to reach out to calm him down.

"What was it like?" Ian begged.

Elijah looked at him and smiled.

"Lucky I had some garlic and artificial butter," he whispered.

"Oh, no. You didn't . . ."

"He sure did look like a giant snail to me. Tell me, Ian, have you ever had a hundred-kilo escargot?"

"By heavens, Ian, he's sick."

Ian looked across at Ellen and nodded in affirmation. "But that's not the question we're dealing with, Ellen."

"I don't give a good god damn what you think we're dealing with, I think we should put him under sedation, turn about, and head for home. And another thing, we should let the Exploration Board come back out here and figure out what the hell is going on with this Father, or whatever it is those people over there are worshiping." Ellen waved her hand off in the direction of Delta Sag.

"First off, I'm not going to sedate Elijah as long as his behavior is reasonable."

"Reasonable, my ass, that madman came up to me and asked if we had any fresh meat. He even pinched my leg. Good Lord, Ian, he gives me the creeps."

"Reasonable, my ass," Richard whispered *sotto voce* to Stasz. "I'd like to see him take a bite out of her buns, she might enjoy it."

"Shut up, pig! Remember I saved your butt from the IFF."

"And I remember in some detail what yours looked like. Stasz, you should have seen it, a little heavy perhaps, but still worth a—"

"Shut up, all of you," Ian shouted. "We've got to make a decision, damn it!"

"Look, Ian," Ellen interjected, "this was originally conceived of as a way for the Chancellor to get rid of some nonconformist or incompetent faculty members."

"Yes indeed," Richard interrupted. "But do speak for yourself, Ellen dearest, when deciding which of the two."

"Give her a chance, will you?" Ian replied, amazed at himself for defending Ellen against Richard's barbs.

Choosing to ignore his comments, she continued.

"I was also going to say that this is an academic mission. We were to establish contact if possible with one or more colonies and find out what happened. Look, Ian, we can't even *gather* any more data. Our memory banks are crammed to capacity, to enter even one more item requires us to dump something else. There's enough data in there to keep our respective professions busy for the next century. Ian, we can go back home, we can go back as heroes, and screw the Chancellor."

Ian shot Richard a glance to suppress the obvious retort.

"I know you want to get back home, too," Ian said, looking at Richard.

Richard merely shook his head and smiled. "I want to see how this argument turns out."

"And you, Stasz?"

"They've got beam weapons—look what they did to that out there." He pointed at the wreckage that drifted just outside their forward viewport.

"So that means you'd prefer to turn back?"

"Look, Ian, it's been fun. I've racked up six months of translight time. By the time we get back, I figure I can take standard retirement plus ten percent. Do you think I want to blow my retirement checks just to go visit the followers of a crazy man dead for the last thousand years?"

"But your curiosity is there, isn't it?"

Stasz shifted uncomfortably, so that he floated out of his couch. "Don't ruin the image of indifference that I've tried to cultivate."

"And, Richard, what do you have to say?" Ian asked, turning away from Stasz.

"The arguments for turning back are obvious. Smith's people are armed and have twice proven their madness. Confrontation with them is something I think is totally beyond our capacity. We already have a valuable cargo of data, which I think should take precedence at this stage of the mission."

Ellen gave an audible sigh of relief.

"But . . ." It was Richard who was prompting.

"Yes, the but," Ian replied. "There're two buts here. We can go back home and turn over this investigation to the bureaucracy. I want you to think about that. Think about our beloved Chancellor. For that matter, think about most any bureaucrat you've ever known. When presented with a problem like this, what will they do? For that matter, what does any bureaucrat excel at?"

"They'll screw it up," Stasz replied.

"That's my point," Ian said softly. "Out toward Delta Sag there is one hell of a mystery, and I fear what someone like the Chancellor and his kind would do to that situation. I'd rather have a group of half-assed intellectuals like ourselves in the driver's seat. And this might sound strange coming from old Ian Lacklin, but damn me, I'm just plain curious. This journey has scared me from day one. It's still scaring me, but I guess I'm getting used to it. We've come this far, I think it's worth the risk to take the final step. The historian in me is dying to know just what really happened to Franklin Smith's people."

"Let's hope you don't die finding out," Stasz replied.

The others fell silent; Ian nodded to each and floated out of the room to his small retreat in the aft storage area. Reaching into his pocket, he pulled out the rod that Elijah had given him. He couldn't tell any of them the real reason that he wanted the expedition to continue, at least not yet.

Even more than finding out about Smith, he now wanted to find out about the alien who came for dinner. If one alien was in the area, there might be another. Ian only hoped that he found them before Smith did. Elijah had been unable to enter the alien's ship, which apparently disappeared while its pilot was becoming dinner for one. Ian thought it might have been launched by a dead-man switch hidden in the alien's equipment or by a timing circuit in the autopilot. The only thing to survive their first encounter was the small cylinder Elijah said had been carried in a metal holster on the alien's carapace. Ian didn't want to consider the possible consequences of Smith's people having the first contact with another civilization. First contact, that is, if one didn't consider Elijah. But how would Smith react to the visitors from Earth? . . . Ian again examined the strange artifact in his hand. It did look somewhat like a swizzle stick with a blue button on top, but he had yet to work up the nerve to press down on that button. Considering where they would be in a matter of hours, he suddenly realized that the only evidence of intelligent nonhuman civilization should be safely stored away. And he knew the perfect place. While the arguments continued up forward, he poked around in Richard's affects and placed the object in his comrade's portable drinking kit. The artifact fitted in like it had been made to match.

"Ready for translight," Stasz called.

"'And who will turn back from the greatest hunt of all,'" Elijah shouted as the faint tremor of the overdrive system began.

Ian opened his eyes for a moment to look forward. Delta Sag was straight ahead, its Doppler shift already noticeable. Soon the jump would kick in completely and radical distort would slide its light through the visible spectrum. The jump would be a short one, then their destination would no longer be a mere pinpoint of light, a distant star. For the first time in over half a year, their cabin would again be flooded with the light of a sun.

The jump shifted up with Stasz's shouted reminder of the chance of breakup. Ian leaned forward, his stomach rebelling in protest.

CHAPTER 11

Automated Archival Unit 2

First Completion Date: 2087

Primary Function: Archival. A farsighted effort instituted
by the United Nations Historical Preservation Organization. Having evaluated the prospects for war, a
multinational team set out to provide as complete
a record as possible of the history of mankind on
Earth. Replicas of all major works of art were produced, all major libraries were copied. The data was
placed aboard four units, two of which were successfully launched from Earth orbit only days before
the first nuclear exchange of the Holocaust War.

Evacuation Date: August 1, 2087.

Overall Design: O'Neill Cylinder, 400 meters by 100 meters. Minimal life-support systems. Design was to be
largely self-sustaining and self-navigating.

Propulsion: Plasma Drive.

Course: SETI Anomaly One.
Political/Social Orientation: None.

"We've locked onto that signal, Ian. It's just come out of occultation by a gas giant, four A.U. ahead. There's strong background interference from a number of radio sources closer in to Delta."

"Shelley, which unit is the beacon from?"

"Ian, it's *Archival 2*!" The tone of her voice caused the others to turn and look in her direction. Ian was already pushing forward to peer over her shoulder at the display screen.

"The jackpot!"

Ian and Shelley started to hug each other, and in her enthusiasm Shelley planted a long kiss on Ian that had the others clapping and cheering.

"All right, all right," Richard said, his curiosity no longer capable of being contained, "what's *Archival 2*? Is it Smith's unit?"

"No, it's just the mother lode of a historical dream. It's the archive ship, launched just before the war. It contains *everything*, Richard. Everything you could imagine. The only complete record of everything from before the war. Good lord, Beaulieu will kiss my feet just for the chance to look at it, just to touch it for one minute. We'll be blowing our noses on honorary doctorates for this!" Ian floated out of the room weeping with joy.

"I guess that means we go to *Archival 2*," Stasz said quietly with an attempt at understatement.

"Stasz, you said you were picking up a lot of background interference. What is it?"

"Oh, only a broad spectrum of interference from a large number of radio frequencies—what you'd pick up in near-Earth space. You know, a first-class civilization, billion-plus-people level of communication . . ." His voice trailed off.

"I think we better tell Ian," Ellen replied, her anxiety now obvious.

"You'll get an argument over it," Stasz responded. "That mad historian wants his archival unit first."

"Where are the signals centered?" Richard asked.

"In toward Delta Sag. Initial printout indicates a small planetary body; it all seems to be coming primarily from that one source."

"Anything from the region of *Archival 2*?"

"Nothing."

"Fine then," Richard replied. "Originally we had planned to stay out here and monitor them for several weeks before we made the move. But let's get into *Archival 2* instead. He'll see the wealth of information there, the historian in him will want to preserve it at all costs, and, I daresay, we'll be hauling back to Earth with the news within a day—this Franklin Smith adventure forgotten. So, let's go on in."

Stasz gave a grunt of assertion, and even Shelley seemed satisfied with Richard's conclusion.

Elijah sat in the back of the cabin, silent, staring at the ball of light whose heavily filtered globe now filled the monitor.

"Hard dock."

Ian was out of his seat and pushing off for the airlock, calling for the others to follow.

Within minutes he was suited up and urging on Shelley and Ellen, acting like a little boy whose parents refuse to get out of bed on Christmas morning.

Stasz came back to join them, and from a small attaché case he produced three stun pistols.

"Ian, you better take these along, just in case."

"Stasz, there hasn't been anyone aboard that vessel since it launched a thousand years ago."

"Bull. This thing's in orbit when it should be heading for the galactic core, that beacon is in perfect working order, and we've picked up strong transmissions from only ten A.U. away. They've been here, Ian, they might be in there now."

"Well, if that's the case, I guess we'll just have to talk it out when we meet them."

"They didn't talk it out when I met them," Elijah said.

Ian looked around at the rest of the crew.

"Look, I know you're not too thrilled about this. I'm just going in to confirm what's in there. If it really is *Archival 2*, I think that information takes higher precedence over anything else. We'll see what we can take back with us, then we get the hell out of here. Does that satisfy everybody?"

The rest were silent.

"Give me the damn guns and let's get going."

And then he thought again of Smith. "I'll be with you in a moment, I forgot something."

"Come on, Ian," Shelley called, "this isn't the time to go to the bathroom."

But he was already out of the chamber. Several minutes later he reappeared, and without another word he motioned them into the airlock.

If Smith did board them, Ian hoped he had now provided the insurance policy. He had pushed five of the six activation switches on the thermomine. If they were threatened with boarding, simply pushing down on the sixth and pulling it back up would finish the job.

The inner airlock to the unit opened effortlessly, and Ian, followed by Ellen, Shelley, and Richard, floated into an open expanse of corridor.

"Oxygen check looks good, Ian," Shelley reported. "No toxicity readings."

With a sigh of relief he pulled off his helmet. He had always hated the claustrophobic things anyhow.

"Look, Ian, that plaque."

He pushed off gently and came up against a plaque of

gold set into the far wall; reaching out with his suction holders, he clamped onto the wall like a spider.

He started to tremble as he read the first line in Old English.

Automated Archival Unit 2
Launch Date 2087
"So that only the best of our world may be remembered."

The same phrase was repeated in half a dozen other languages, beneath that was a small directory and map giving directions to the vast interior storage areas.

"This is it, Shelley, this is it!"

"It looks like the catalog directory is over this way," Ellen called, her apprehensions momentarily forgotten in the enthusiasm for what they had found.

The other three followed her as she floated along the docking corridor and stepped into a slowly rotating stairwell that led down to the rotating mass of the cylinder.

At first they simply let themselves drop down the shaft, but with the gradual increase in acceleration, they soon grabbed hold of the handrailings to break what could have developed into a disastrous fall.

Another gold plaque pointed them into a dimly lit corridor that was lined with racks of filing cards.

"Now that's curious," Ellen whispered. "It's the precomputer method of filing data. I remember reading about it. Seems awfully cumbersome."

"Logical though," Ian replied. "They must have a computer master, but this was included in case of a total power failure. Look over there."

He pointed to a brightly painted circle where several dozen large books were laid out side by side.

Ian approached the books and stared at them with eager anticipation, the way some people approach a gourmet meal or the first night with a new lover.

"Ian, come over here and look at this," Shelley cried. "Good Lord, just look at what they have!"

Shelley was waving a small filing card over her head, which she had, in her enthusiasm, plucked out of one of the filing cabinets.

Ian came over to her side and examined her find. "I remember you talking about the old Apollo missions," she shouted, "so I saw this cabinet with *Ap-As* listed on it. Here's a card that lists an *Apollo 8*. Level Three, Room 224, File 203-090-112–130. Ian, they don't have one Apollo card in there, they have half a hundred!"

The four of them looked at each other and within seconds they were all busy digging into the files, each one looking for his or her favorite topic, exploring the answer to a question from the world of the past that had forever puzzled them.

Ian was overwhelmed. He thought the discovery of the library aboard the longevity unit had been the find of lifetime, but this was simply beyond his comprehension. In simple awe of it all, he started to weep. He had found the Valhalla of historians at last!

Hours later he staggered back to the filing area, leaving the others to the enthusiastic examination of the finds. There was enough sense still about him to realize that this unit had not been vacant for the last millennium. First off, something had altered its course from the original route into the galactic core. Second, something had provided the data to this vessel and had guided it into orbit. Finally, there was significant evidence of repair and maintenance.

He was drawn back at last to the books set off in the white circle. They were obviously set there to draw a visitor's attention. Not sure what to anticipate, Ian reached over and opened the first book.

He suddenly realized that Shelley had come up to his side.

"What is it?"

"I think it's a translator. Look, the pictographs for a man and a woman. Here's a diagram of our solar system and a map giving our location in relationship to the rest of the galaxy. That's it—these books are a translator for anyone, or anything, for that matter, who might find this ship."

"Ian? Stasz here."

There was a note of anxiety in his voice.

"Go on."

"Ian, I've just picked up a high-energy burst from the forward antenna of *Archival 2*. Damn near blew me out of my couch."

"I think we just hit the doorbell," Ian said softly. "Richard, Ellen, did you hear that? Meet me back in the catalog area before we head out."

Within the minute Stasz was back with more news.

"I've just locked on to several incoming energy sources. I can't tell what they are yet, but they were in high orbit around this planet. They're accelerating like mad. Damn it, you people better hurry!"

A doorway at the far end of the corridor slid open and Ellen burst through it panting for breath. "Where's Richard, I want to get moving!"

"Richard, how long before you get back here?" Ian tried to sound calm, but he knew his nervousness was showing.

"Another five minutes, at least, Ian. I'm way the hell at the other end of this ship."

Damn it! Ian silently cursed himself. He had screwed up. He should have had everybody stay together. He got so carried away by the honey pot that he had not thought of the consequences.

"Ian. Look, why don't you people head on out without me? Ahh, I mean you'll stand a better chance that way."

"What is this, Richard, a god-damn video drama? Cut the garbage and move your fat butt up here."

He could hear the audible sigh of relief.

"I hoped you'd say that, but at least my offer sounded good."

"You'd never have made it if I was in command," Ellen muttered.

"Ian, you have two minutes. They've already started to decelerate. For God's sake, get moving!"

Richard finally burst through the far door, gasping for breath and looking as if he was on the verge of an apoplectic fit.

"Let's go!"

Ellen took off at a run, while Shelley and Ian fell in on either side of the exhausted physician.

Reaching the stairway, they pushed Richard ahead of them while he cursed them and begged pitifully for a moment to regain his breath.

"Ian, I've got them on visual, there's three of them. They're about our size but look like they're armed, a couple of old-style missiles slung under each of them."

"Stasz, can we punch through to translight from a standing start?"

"Increases the breakup possibilities by a factor of ten. I must remind you that you never liked the odds to start with."

"Screw the odds; power the damn thing up."

"One of them is swinging into the opposite docking port, Ian. This doesn't look good at all..." There was a high-pitched shriek of static and then nothing.

"Do you think they hit him?" Shelley cried.

"If they had, we would have felt the vibration run through the ship. I think they're just jamming him. Come on, Richard, move it!"

They were rapidly moving into the low-gravity region and finally, in exasperation, Ian braced himself on the ladder and leaned onto Richard's backside, giving him a tremendous shove.

Richard arched up and away like a champagne cork popping out of a bottle. With a crash he slammed into the bulkhead on the other side of the stairwell and ricocheted out into the main zero-gravity corridor. Ian and Shelley were right behind him.

They pushed off for the opposite end, where their own docking port was located. Ellen was already there and waving them on.

Just another twenty meters to go and suddenly Ian felt a slight shifting in the air, as if a distant doorway had been opened. Grabbing a handrail, he looked back the way they had come. Another docking port was open. A shadowy figure filled the bay, and Ian felt a tremor of fear. They had lost the race.

Trying to smile, he raised his hand and tossed the stun pistol away. The figure he was facing had some far heavier artillery.

"Ahh, greetings, friend," he said in a high, squeaky voice. "Ahh ... We've come in peace for all mankind. How's that?"

The blast knocked him over backward, slamming him into darkness.

CHAPTER 12

Exile Base 11; Alpha/Omega
First Completion Date: 2078
Primary Function: Adopting an old Russian concept, the
United States started exiling political dissidents to space
in 2068. On the eve of the Holocaust War several
hundred thousand "political unreliables, conscientious
objectors, and disarmament activists," led by Dr.
Franklin Smith, were exiled to space.
Evacuation Date: Believed to be August 7, 2087, the recorded date of the primary exchange between the Third
World powers versus the United States and Soviet Re-
publics.
Overall Design: O'Neill Cylinder. Four kilometers by 800
meters. All exile bases were populated far more densely
than the maximum potential carrying capabilities. Thus
the units were dependent on Earth for life support. It
is believed by Beaulieu that no exile unit could have

survived longer than six months after departure from near-Earth, due to depletion of resources.

Propulsion: Ion Drive with nuclear pulse backup.

Course: SETI Anomaly One.

Political/Social Orientation: Penal system, largely self-governing, but managed by USNSC (United States Near Space Council). Departure in fact was hoped for and encouraged by Earthside government as a means of eliminating political dissent without having actually to kill the opposition.

"I'd prefer if you moved that thing from the back of my head. You can see I've brought you where you wanted."

Stasz's words echoed through Ian's consciousness, each syllable like a hammer on an anvil. He wasn't sure yet if he wanted to open his eyes, since he was still debating if he was dead or alive.

"Croce, you fat slob, we should have left you behind," Ellen said in a shrill voice. "We could have jumped out in time, but, oh no, Ian had to be the hero, so now we're all stuck."

If he was dead, then he must be in Hell. He opened his eyes and looked around.

"Well, our fearless historian is wide awake at last," Richard said, offering him a tumbler. He chortled softly then beckoned for Ian to look forward. Ian gladly accepted.

The couch normally occupied by Shelley was now held by a stranger. From the back, Ian saw broad shoulders and an erect carriage. His hair was tied back in a simple queue that hung over the back of the couch—the color of it nearly matching his dark, full features. In his left hand was a pistol, which he held to the back of Stasz's head.

"Two more of his buddies are in the back checking," Richard cautioned, "so I wouldn't suggest trying anything."

"For God sake, Ian, don't try anything," Shelley whispered. "They hit you with a stunner. But this guy's got an old-fashioned powder-driven pistol. Don't get him mad, for God's sake!"

"Where's Elijah?"

"I sedated him," Richard replied. "After they hit you, Ellen, Shelley, and I kind of thought it best to go along peaceful like. We let them into our ship and Elijah nearly went wild. I was afraid they'd kill him, so I just came up and jabbed him one from behind. He'll be out for another couple of hours."

"Where are they taking us?"

The guard turned back and looked at Ian with an almost pleasant smile. "Just for a little talk. The priests of the Father will want to hear your story."

To Ian the language sounded like modified Old English. "The Father?" he asked cautiously.

The guard smiled, but this time with a sinister light in his eyes. "When you say 'the Father,' be sure to say it with the proper respect."

"Oh yes, of course, but of course."

"Coming up on jump-down," Stasz announced evenly. "Remember, friend, you might get sick, but don't blame me."

"Ten seconds, five . . ."

"Will you look at that!" Stasz pointed ahead and then to the left and the right. For the moment he had forgotten that his life was held by a stranger in the couch next to him.

To his surprise Ian found that his stomach had managed to survive jump-down intact. Perhaps it had something to do with the short duration of the jump, but that question was pushed from his mind as he looked out the forward viewing ports. It took him several seconds to grasp the perspective and scale of what he was seeing.

"It must be a hundred kilometers long," Ian whispered.

"Yes, kilometers," their guard said. "The one forward is large, but you wish to go to that one there." And he pointed to what looked like an old, familiar design. An O'Neill cylinder, probably the original, but it was simply dwarfed by the hundreds of others that filled the heavens in every direction.

They were in high orbit above a deeply pitted surface, and as Ian examined it, he realized that a significant portion of the planet was scarred and torn, as if a giant had gnawed on it.

"Each one of those units could provide for well over a million people," Shelley said softly.

Good heavens, Ian thought, the population must number in the billions.

Following the guard's directions, Stasz guided *Discovery* through ever-increasing traffic. Finally, taking the control headset, the guard called for docking clearance. Within minutes the *Discovery* was lined up for final approach.

For the moment Ian had forgotten his fears as he contemplated the myriad designs of the shipping around him. He felt as if he had arrived at an odd Sargasso Sea, where ships of every conceivable design had collected. As the *Discovery* turned in on final, the ship slowly rotated on its X-axis so that a full sweep of local space was given to the travelers, and all were overawed by the sheer sizes and numbers.

"Our biggest is nearly a hundred and fifty kilometers in length," the guard said, his pride in such an accomplishment obvious. But it was the only information he would volunteer to them.

"We've got a hard dock," Stasz said as the faint vibration of contact ran through the vessel.

"Very good. I'm glad I was not forced to kill you." The guard smiled and holstered his pistol.

"So am I," Stasz replied weakly.

"You see," the guard said mockingly, "I wouldn't know

how to pilot this ship." Laughing uproariously, he made his way aft, beckoning for them to follow.

"Maybe they all have a sense of humor," Shelley said hopefully.

"Ask Elijah about that," Ian replied.

The guard stopped by the airlock door and, turning, faced his prisoners. "Go get the crazy one and bring him with you."

Taking a still-wobbly Elijah in tow, they went through the first airlock and waited for the door to the other ship to open.

"Bear yourselves with dignity," the guard said evenly, "for you walk upon sacred ground."

The doorway closed behind them.

"Sounds like we're going to church," Richard said sarcastically.

"Shut up," Ian said. "To these people, I think it is."

The doorway slid open to a tunnel of darkness. A single hooded form awaited them. "Follow me," it commanded.

Ian shrugged, pushed off, keeping Elijah in tow, and the others followed.

The hooded form drifted down a darkened corridor, his long black robes billowing out around him so that he had the appearance of a dark ghost, drifting weightlessly through the night. Reaching the end of the corridor, the ghostly guide pointed toward an open elevator. The six went into the cubicle and their guide came in after them. It was impossible to make out his features beneath the hooded robe, and their guide was silent as he beckoned for them to grasp the handholds as the elevator dropped away underneath them. Within seconds the first wispy pull of gravity took hold, and their feet drifted to the floor. Ian judged that they were in, at best, a quarter-gravity zone. When the elevator stopped, its doors opened into a large, softly lit chamber that appeared to be an audience hall.

"Go forward and wait," the guide commanded in a cold, mechanical voice.

They meekly obeyed. Elijah was starting to awaken from his drugged state, and Richard urgently whispered a plea for him to keep his mouth shut and not to make any sudden moves.

As their eyes adjusted to the dim light, they saw that a low dais rose at the far end of the chamber. In the center of the dais a single chair was occupied by yet another hooded form.

"In the name of the Father, come forward." This one's tone was not threatening but it held a definite air of command.

As they drew closer, Ian realized that their host was not alone. Several dozen others were sitting on the floor before and to either side of the dais.

Ian was, of all things, reminded of several prints he had seen of ancient Japanese warriors sitting cross-legged in front of their warlord. As he drew closer, the comparison took on even more similarity; to his amazement most of the hooded forms had swords that were laid on the floor in front of them. All were wearing the same dark flowing robes that their guide aboard the ship had worn. There was no ornamentation, no design or emblem to be seen, except for the one who sat upon the low, backless chair in the center—his robe was of a soft, shimmering white that contrasted with the black robes of those who sat before him.

There was a soft, gentle sound in the darkness that reminded Ian of wind chimes. The sound brought back for a moment sharp clear memories of summer evenings, and the memory hurt with a piercing blow. Ian half wondered if these people had somehow read into his memory and used that sound to provoke such thoughts.

Ian and his comrades approached to the edge of the dais and, as if by instinct, Ian knew that it would be an insult for them to step upon it. He stopped and the others drew up around him. He prayed fervently that Elijah would keep still, for he half suspected that they would leave the room in only one of two conditions, and he had no desire to fall into the second category.

Farthest to the right, a hooded form stood, belted his sword, and walked to the center of the dais. Bowing to the white-robed figure, the form pulled back its hood and turned to face them.

"Where are you from?"

Ian was surprised to hear her high, clear voice, and he was struck by her uncommon beauty—dark ebony skin, sharply chiseled features, and long flowing hair.

He hesitated for a second.

"Do I take your hesitation as an unwillingness to answer?"

He better act quickly. "Ahh, no . . . I'm not sure of your dialect, that's all."

"Your language roots are Old American," Ellen interrupted, "the same as ours, but its pronunciations are different from ours. But we'll learn soon enough."

Ian was glad for the momentary interruption. He had to think out his answer.

"Then I repeat, where are you from?"

"Your ancestral home, the Earth."

"You've mastered faster-than-light?"

"That's right," Ian replied. "We have faster-than-light capability."

There was a faint murmur from the others. He realized that most of them were male, but there was a fair proportion of females, as well.

"How long ago did you leave Earth?"

"I'm not sure of our mutual time measurements. Do you still measure things in what are called years?"

She pondered this for a moment and then nodded her head. "Yes, years. I understand what that is. I am thirty-one years."

"It took us one-half a year to arrive here, with nearly a month of stopovers at other places."

The excitement was evident—the others turned one to the other and Ian felt as if a basic law of decorum had been broken by this display of emotions.

Another dark-robed figure stood up, sword in hand, and the hall fell silent.

"You are born of the Earth?" he said with a deep, resonant voice.

"Yes, you see, we've come..." Ian looked at Richard and let the ridiculous words die.

"Then you are unclean. You are born of those who persecuted us, you are born of those against whom we have declared jihad by the will of the Father. You are born of those who cursed and abandoned us. Your blood shall be spilled, your carcasses abandoned in the night."

He took another step forward and unsheathed his sword. "Cleanse this place of their filth, their sacrilege!" he shouted, bringing the blade back in preparation for a two-handed blow.

Ian jumped backward in a desperate attempt to avoid the flashing blade.

"Fire and Hell, what's wrong with ye?" Elijah called. He stepped forward and confronted the swordsman. "Strike, but 'for hate's sake I spit my last breath at thee!'"

There was a murmur of approval from the others, and the swordsman, turning his wrath from Ian, now prepared to swing a decapitating blow at Elijah.

"Nara." The white-robed form was out of his seat, and the others turned to look at him.

"Nara, be still. Sit. You disgrace yourself with such show."

Nara turned, his whole form trembling.

"Gregor, so what if the Father is awakening. He knows not the situation now; I do, and so do others. Even you know and wonder why he must be awakened."

"Be still!" Gregor screamed. He looked to the others

and saw that most of them were nodding in response to Nara's words.

"Let the Father speak for the Father. They are unclean, yes, but to kill them"—he swept them with a gaze of contempt—"that can wait."

Ian was suddenly aware that Shelley was clinging to his arm.

Nara stood with blade drawn, his gaze now fixed on the white-robed master. With a blinding flash he swung the blade in a backhanded swing that whisked within a fraction of Elijah's face, and sheathed his blade. With a low bow to Gregor, he strode out of the room. And again there was a murmur from the rest of the assembly. Gregor turned to his right and nodded to the two sitting closest to him.

"Go and help his honor," he said softly. And wordlessly they stood and left the room.

"You, fat one. Are you so typical of those who we thought were so fearless?"

Ian had a hard time finding his voice, and he suddenly realized that his body was covered in a cold sweat. "Yes."

"This bears great thought. Next—is it truth that you have the ability to go beyond light?"

Ian could merely nod.

"Don't tell him anything," Elijah hissed.

"Silence! I could kill you with a word."

"You killed me fifty years ago. I am arisen from that silent death. You cannot kill me ever again, for I am already dead."

"A holy fool," someone muttered from the shadows. "It is written then that he should be spaced."

"He will be spaced when I command," Gregor replied. "Now, you who are called Ian, do you understand how this vessel can do such a thing?"

"Ahh, well, to be honest, no."

Gregor drew closer. "If I think that you lie, I'll slit your throat and then cut out your tongue and jam it down your windpipe."

Ian was aware that a puddle was forming around his shoes. "I don't know how it works."

"Then tell me which of you knows how it does."

"No, I'll not betray a friend."

Gregor looked him in the eye and held his gaze.

"You have more courage than it appears," Gregor snapped. "The mystery of your coming requires more examination, for I see the dream of our jihad come to fruition at last with such a device that you now possess. This requires far more decision than I am capable of. You shall live, for the moment."

Gregor turned away.

There was a murmur of angry voices in the room.

"Silence. I like it not, but the Father is already awakening. I cannot exceed my mandate, even if I wish it. He must be awakened."

"But, Gregor," came a voice from the back of the room, "take the burden yourself this time and let him return to sleep."

"Speak not or I shall force upon you what Nara has earned."

Suddenly the two men who had followed Nara returned to the room and walked to his side.

"Did Nara keep his honor?" Gregor asked.

One of the two held up his blade for all to see—a dark substance dripped from the tip of the weapon. The others murmured their approval.

"He had already cut himself open by the time we arrived. I ended for him as second, so he would not cry out and thus be shamed. Nara's honor was preserved."

The others expressed their approval and, to Ian's ears, sounded happy.

"Then it is time to take communion with Nara's honor," Gregor intoned ceremonially. "Let these others be taken to a place of waiting, for the Father must be prayed to: A decision must be made."

They were led away by their female interrogator, and as he watched them while leaving the room, Ian had a bad feeling about what a "communion with Nara's honor" really meant.

Ian looked over to Elijah and saw that he was smiling hungrily.

"Well, this is another fine mess you've gotten us into, Ian," Ellen said wearily.

Ian looked up at Ellen and smiled weakly.

"Can't you lay off him for a little while?" Stasz interjected.

"Why are you defending him all of a sudden?"

"Because I have a feeling all our butts are going to be fried in this one, and in spite of his screw-up in bringing us here, I have to say he really hasn't done all that bad."

Ian looked up at Stasz and nodded his thanks.

Richard and Shelley were asleep on a low cot set into the far corner of the room. His heavy arm was draped protectively over Shelley's shoulder, but she didn't seem to mind and had drifted off to sleep hours ago.

How long they had been in the holding cell was only a guess. It had already been indicated to them that their respective roles had easily been ascertained by a search of the *Discovery*, and after that one bit of communication, not another word of information had been exchanged.

Much to Ian's surprise, they had been allowed their personal possessions, so he had his pocket computer and the alien artifact, which he had quickly explained as a religious medallion.

Only Elijah seemed unperturbed by the situation. He was explaining that "to be locked up with even one other person is my idea of paradise," when the door to their cell opened noiselessly. Only a single guard stood there—

the white-robed one they had called Gregor. He pointed to Ian then beckoned for him to follow.

Ian suddenly felt as if the decision over their fate had been made. They must have discovered by now the operational and repair manuals stored in the ship's computers. With just a little research work they should be able to replicate the *Discovery*; therefore there was no need any longer for the Earthmen's "unclean" bodies to be kept alive.

Ian stood up and attempted to maintain his dignity. He gently shook hands with Stasz and Elijah and lightly touched Ellen on the shoulder.

"Should I wake up Richard and Shelley?" Ellen asked. There was a choke in her voice.

He shook his head. "I don't think I could handle the upset; you better not. If I don't come back, tell Shelley I really regret not sleeping with her. It's been hard not to, but tell her I fought down the nearly overwhelming desire because I didn't want to create any friction aboard ship." He tried to chuckle.

Ian looked at Ellen and smiled. "Maybe I should have made a pass at you, as well."

"Go on, get out of here." She turned away.

Ian walked out of the room and Gregor beckoned for him to proceed down the corridor.

"Are you going to kill me?" Ian suddenly asked.

"We all die. Death is an illusion, only honor and name remain. When you die, Ian Lacklin, try to leave more behind than a puddle on the floor."

Suspecting that Gregor was laughing, Ian looked back over his shoulder, but his features were solemn and Ian realized that he had been perfectly serious.

"I do not hate you, Ian Lacklin, but I would not gain honor by slaying thee. I know that there is honor in you, in spite of what your outward appearance might tell. Gain honor and then the slaying of you would be worthy for one such as myself."

What the hell is this guy talking about? Ian wondered. If gaining honor is the ticket to this man's sword, then forget it.

"I know what you are thinking, Ian Lacklin, but I believe that you will understand, as well, and will in the end embrace your honor and die for it."

Gregor touched Ian on the shoulder and motioned for him to stop.

The chimelike sound that Ian had heard in the audience hall was drifting on the edge of hearing, but his attention was diverted by the procession coming his way from the other end of the corridor. Gregor backed to the wall and Ian followed his example to let the procession pass. They numbered nearly a hundred, each of them robed. Some were dark as ebony, others paler, a few had Gregor's Asiatic features. It seemed as if half a dozen races had been blended together during the millennium and a composite of all had been melded into one, with the black having a slight dominance. They walked with a certain assured grace, male and female alike. Not one looked sidelong at him, so perfect was their discipline.

After the procession's passage Gregor again pointed forward, and Ian tried to somehow emulate those who had just passed by—walking to his death without a whine.

Finally they stopped at the audience chamber where Ian had been received earlier. He looked at Gregor questioningly. Was his death then to be a spectacle before an audience?

Gregor pointed to the door, which slid open as if guided by unseen hands.

"Is this to be my end?"

Like an angel of death, Gregor silently pointed, his robed and hooded figure surreal and nightmarish.

"Answer me, at least let me know. Am I to die in there?"

Still there was no response.

"Well, then I have one thing to say if that's the case."

Again Gregor beckoned for him to go.

Ian screwed up his courage, trying to remember his best Old English, hoping that the words still meant the same even in this culture.

"Well then, if that's the case, then fuck you!"

Turning on his heels, he strode through the doorway.

"Marvelous, absolutely marvelous." The voice was deep and melodious.

The door slid closed behind Ian, and in the semidarkness he could make out but one figure on the dais. Ian strode closer, and the figure stood up as if in greeting.

"I haven't heard it said that way in nearly a thousand years. And with just the right inflection!"

Ian stopped in front of the dais and looked up.

"Yes, Ian Lacklin. My name is Dr. Franklin Smith."

CHAPTER 13

Nearly six and a half feet tall, he towered over Ian and beneath his simple robe was a powerful build. His chocolate features were wreathed in a salt-and-pepper beard that matched his bushy hair.

Smith stepped closer to Ian and gave him a hard, appraising stare that seemed to slice into his soul. Ian tried to hold Smith's gaze, but after a brief painful struggle, he broke off the one-sided contest of wills.

"Ah, yes." Smith turned away from Ian and walked back up to the dais, regaining the seat occupied in the last interview by Gregor. Smith pointed to the far corner of the dais.

"There's a chair over there. Fetch it and come sit before me."

"Should I kneel first or something like that?"

"Very good, Ian, very good. But if any of my people heard that comment in that tone, you'd be dead before even I could stop them." He paused for a moment then stared him straight in the eye. "So don't be a wise-ass, or your shit will be cooked."

Ian grabbed the chair and sat down.

Smith was silent for some minutes, and Ian thought it best to let him take the lead in whatever it was that was going to happen.

Still staring straight into his eyes, Smith finally started. "You're a historian, are you not? That's what the ship's records indicate."

"Yes, I'm a historian."

"Then as a historian I know you have a million questions. I have my questions, too, but perhaps they will be answered better if I see what path it is that you choose."

Smith stretched and mumbled a quiet curse while rubbing his back. "Go ahead, historian, ask."

As the fullness of his opportunity washed over him, for a moment Ian was struck speechless. The past was but a dream, a dream lived more richly by any good historian, but still a dream. He thought for a moment that he had touched it with the life-extension colony, but that had turned to the ashes of senility. Yet here sat Franklin Smith, someone out of a past as distant and dead as Ssu-ma Zhung, Hitler, Napoleon, or Clarke. He had read of Smith, had charted his activities during the days leading up to the Holocaust and studied his instrumental role in the grand conspiracy of the colonies to escape disaster. And now he sat across from him. Was it really even him at all? he suddenly wondered, growing suspicious.

"How?"

"How. Ah, yes, how am I here; not forgotten ashes, nor half-remembered legend." He stretched again and leaned forward. "You know, Ian, I suspected that would be your first question. The others"—he waved vaguely, as if indicating the entire universe—"take it as a miracle. But it was nothing more than a damn good research program at U.S.C. Have you heard of U.S.C.?"

Ian shook his head.

"Not a great school—the Chinese research programs were far better at that point—but still not bad. Well, they had isolated a number of the properties of hibernation. It was on the eve of the war..." His voice trailed off for a moment and he was silent.

He suddenly looked up at Ian with a start. "Just remembering, you see, it really wasn't that long ago for me. Before the war, an old professor of mine who was in on the project was exiled to the life-extension colony. I looked him up afterward. I heard that your records indicate a visit there, as well?"

Ian nodded but said nothing.

"He gave me a number of doses and the antidote for it, in consideration for a favor of mine."

"Such as not destroying the life-extension colony the way you did a couple of the others?"

Smith was silent again, and Ian wondered if he had gone too far. Smith smiled as if in warning, then continued.

"Through the accident of being scheduled in one of his classes while still an undergraduate, and a later chance meeting, I can sit here today, a millennium hence. While he..." His voice trailed off again for a moment. "Well, while he, if unfortunate enough to survive what happened, has long ago been taken by the inevitable thief of life and gone into the darkness.

"So, with such a simple turn of fate, I am injected with the drug and fall into a deep dreamless sleep. It can be for a day, or it can, as in one case, last for over a century— as long as I am occasionally given an intravenous injection and my unsensing limbs are manipulated so that they do not atrophy. A century, I said, and to my body not a month has passed. When there is need for me, I am wakened by the antidote. And so it was that Gregor, whose grandfather had once so served me, decided that I should be called, so that I might judge for myself what it is that you bring to me."

"And the passage of the centuries is nothing then to you?"

"The leave-taking, the war, the first months of madness are not two years past for me. A millennium, Ian Lacklin, is as if only yesterday. This long inexorable journey but a brief flicker in time. Your wondrous machine, Ian Lacklin, which has taken the journey of over fifty generations and compressed it into a moment, does in some ways compare with the journey that I have taken, as well. You remember Earth as it is today. And I, I have memories just as fresh, but of an Earth now gone for a thousand years."

He chuckled sadly in that rich, full voice.

"Only one question answered so far, Ian Lacklin. There must be yet ten thousand more."

He was right, and Ian wondered for a moment if the conversation could just continue forever, postponing what he feared was the inevitable order for his death.

"I know that you've had contact with several colonies from Earth, but you haven't run into anything else? You know, contact of some kind?"

"You mean an alien civilization?"

Ian nodded.

"We've picked up some signals, most from the original SETI point. I was told there was one quite close not a generation ago, but so far, Ian, nothing. Why do you ask?"

"Oh, just curious, that's all."

Smith looked at Ian closely, as if he suspected something, so Ian quickly pushed ahead with another question.

"I know the how of your cheating death and time. But why?"

"Wouldn't you cheat it? Think for a moment, Ian Lacklin. How long does the average man now live on Earth?"

"Three score is pretty good."

"Ah, yes, I imagine the aftereffects of the war. Before that madness came, we were averaging a full century on Earth. Some aboard the geriatric units were approaching a century and a half."

"On the life-extension unit many have passed the millennium mark," Ian replied, "but it wasn't a very pretty sight."

"Yes, yes, I can imagine. But as I was saying, suppose you could be given the chance to go to sleep and awaken for one or two days in each of the centuries to come—down through the ages, forever seeing what new and wondrous things would await us in our future. Wouldn't you take it?"

Ian could only agree, but underneath it all he imagined that it would be exciting and terribly empty—to awaken each time in a world where he knew no one. He sensed something else; a faint glimmer of excitement shone in Smith's eyes that wasn't there before.

"But there is another reason, isn't there?"

Franklin smiled. And the smile to Ian was one of threat.

"There is my mission, as well." His voice increased in power, as if he was suddenly addressing a multitude rather than one nervous historian.

"Your mission, you say?"

"Yes, but another time for that, Ian Lacklin. You'll learn soon enough."

Ian sensed that a door had just been closed on a possible line of questioning, at least for the present, so he gathered in his thoughts for a moment and struck out in a new direction.

"According to Beaulieu, you were one of the key figures of the secretive Alpha Psi Council, the group that was instrumental in organizing the plan to evacuate all colonial units."

"Who is this Beaulieu?"

"One of the greatest historians alive today. It was Beaulieu who proved that man first landed on the Moon during the rule of Truman."

"Close enough," Smith muttered.

"He's leading the dig at Base Seven on Mars. The Copernican dig, the one that uncovered all the records of the Great Migration, was initiated by him, as well."

"I knew we should have blown that base as we moved out," Smith said evenly.

Ian didn't bother to follow up on that either but decided to wait for an answer. He could see that Smith was enjoying himself. In a strange way Ian was a contemporary of the near-mythical man, perhaps one of the few people alive who could understand the ramifications and intricacies of Smith's time and place.

"Yes, the Psi Council, as we called it," Smith continued. "I think, Ian, you understand the time and its events. My grandsires had made the Great Leap forward into space—that realm with all its promise and dreams. Then there was my generation, a generation taught to believe that we were the ones who would unbind ourselves forever from the confines of Earth.

"I was born in space, *Unit 333*, my mother a Nigerian linguist, my father an American mission coordinator for a Powersat unit."

Ian was having a hard time understanding some of Smith's monolog but he didn't interrupt. Smith was warming to his subject, his full voice rising and falling as if he were telling a story to a group of young children who were fascinated by every word he said. Ian had his first suspicions that Smith was slightly mad.

"I was sent Earthside and, of all things, it was philosophy that took me. And with it came an Earthside position teaching. Those were hard times, Ian, ripe with a promise. Man could have gone far. But the darkness was already overwhelming us in a world of haves and have-nots. The great rivals of the previous century banded together out of fear of those whom they now had to suppress. The world was carrying a burden of twelve billion souls, Ian. Twelve billion. Once we had dreamed that space could take them. But faster than we could take them off-planet, more were born—and so the madness came.

"I was banished from Earth in seventy-eight, after the Second Arizonan Incident. I had become a leader in a disarmament drive; I and a hundred thousand others, mostly from the southwestern part of our country, were banished to a penal colony. This place here—" He shouted out the words and slammed the arm of the chair that he was sitting in. "One hundred thousand in a unit that could not sustain more than twenty-five thousand in closed-system regime."

He stopped, then smiled softly, like an old man who is concerned that he has just frightened the child he was talking to. Ian smiled back wanly and Smith continued.

"I could see what was coming. The darkness descending. All the nations of Earth would call upon their colonies to join in the nationalistic madness of their mother countries. And such madness! We had been living in space for nearly a century. We of space, from a dozen different nations, had far more in common with each other than with those mad fools below. It had been the same with America when at last her people had realized they were no longer Europeans. And so it was with us. Why should we slaughter each other for the sake of those madmen who were of a dying breed—the last generations of *Homo sapiens*?"

He said "*Homo sapiens*" with a disdain that was frightening.

"We were of the next generation of man!" Smith shouted. "And I knew that in the end it would come down not to a confrontation between the petty nationalistic states but a confrontation between those below and those of us above.

"But we were too weak yet. It would be a hundred years, perhaps a millennium before we would be ready.

"Security at the penal colony was lax, especially for one such as myself who already had a name and was widely known on Earth. A few well-placed bribes and I was allowed a class-one visa for space-to-space flight. Just as long as I did not return below. It was thus that I started to meet with those from the other units and formed the network you call Alpha Psi. It was an open secret—the governments of Earth knew what we were planning from the start. But they needed us, our products, the energy we beamed down, so they did not attempt to stop us from planning and stockpiling the necessary systems that would get us out of there. No one on Earth wanted to force the confrontation. And they assumed, as well, that no unit was one hundred percent self-contained. To the second decimal of the ninety-ninth percentile, yes—but there were still some few items that we needed from Earth on a regular basis. And as you know, a unit is only self-contained to the degree of its first perishable life-sustaining substance.

"But we labored on that, as well. That was our true secret, while we openly prepared in other ways. That is where we pushed our research, and soon we could improve self-sufficiency by a factor of ten. Then the Exodus began. One unit left, and then another, finally it was in the dozens, and then the hundreds. The men of Earth couldn't stop us without forcing a major confrontation. Finally when they worked up the nerve to do it, the end was already upon them."

He smiled sadly and looked off into the distance, as if recalling a half-forgotten dream.

"The Soviet-Pakistani Incident precipitated the first exchange. Even from fifty thousand miles out, we could see the flashes and firestorms. We made our moves as planned—before we ourselves would be dragged into the conflagration—and abandoned Earth to the fate created by those who were too inferior to understand.

"Yes, Ian, I was an Alpha Psi leader. I was the philosopher who motivated the others. We evacuated, Ian Lacklin, but it came far too soon for our unit. I want you to contemplate this, Ian Lacklin. We had one hundred thousand aboard, of which we calculated only twenty-five thousand could be supported by the ecosystem. Contemplate what that meant to us, contemplate what that did to a philosophy professor who was now the appointed leader of a colony doomed to die from overpopulation. I cursed them all. I cursed those who destroyed what might have been, and set me upon this Hegira."

"I'm not sure I understand. What is a hegira?"

"Ah, yes, but of course you wouldn't understand. I am weary, Ian, and shall soon leave you. But don't worry. This conversation shall continue, for I do find it amusing. Yes, the Hegira. When Muhammad the Prophet was not recognized by the fools and unbelievers of Mecca, he and his followers were driven out of the city into exile. That is the time that the True Believers date their calendar from, the Hegira or exile of the Prophet. And so we were driven out, as well, Ian Lacklin—a hegira that has lasted eleven centuries."

Franklin Smith stood up, stretched slowly, and walked past Ian and out toward the far door, his silken robes rustling lightly with his passage.

"My Hegira—which I as the Father have lived through from the beginning. And which now, thanks to you and the present you bring, will soon end with fire and sword."

Ian was alone for three days, as near as he could estimate, before he was allowed to rejoin the others.

Surprisingly their captors had allowed some of their familiar items to be brought back from the *Discovery*, and Richard greeted Ian with a tumbler and a sad lament.

"I had two cases left, two cases, and the bastards only

let me take this one bottle off." And he held up the last precious container, now three-quarters of the way to empty.

"Take it as a great honor and sign of my friendship," Richard said melodramatically, "that I saved this final drink for you." He poured the rest of the contents into the tumbler and offered it to Ian.

"What did they do to the ship?" Ian asked.

Stasz drew closer. "It seems our messiah friend is a little nervous about his catch," he whispered softly. "We were allowed to take off some personal items, but then the ship was sealed."

"Any cargo removed?"

"Nothing that I could see, " Stasz replied. "They did detect the radiation in that old thermomine in the aft storage compartment. That really set them off, and they put a secure lock on the door and left it there."

Ian smiled at this information and reached into his pocket to hold the alien cylinder, as if it were a talisman to ward off evil.

Shelley came to Ian's's side and wrapped her arms around him. For a second he regretted his earlier confession, but he went ahead anyhow and kissed her lightly on the forehead.

"We thought maybe you weren't coming back," Ellen said, a note of concern in her voice.

"We saw him, we did. Saw their great dark Father," Elijah proclaimed. "He invited me to their communion of honor for you. I can hardly wait."

Still not used to Elijah's predilections, Ian backed away from him.

So the friends talked quietly among themselves. Each had met with Smith. With Stasz the talk was technical and dealt with the operation of an overdrive ship. From Stasz's descriptions they all realized he had lied to the point of absurdity with Smith when discussing the defenses of Earth and the limitless fleets of overdrive ships that swarmed the galaxy.

Ian smiled as Richard described their comparisons of medical technology and shook his head sadly. Here was an old friend, lost four-score light-years from home, brought to an early end by his mismanagement. Ian's eyes started to fill, and he looked away.

Ellen said they had spoken of language and culture. She had even asked to use one of her precious survey forms, which she had saved for just such a moment. Smith had laughed and said he would consider it. With Shelley he reminisced about his days as a graduate student.

Only Elijah would not speak of their conversation and, when asked, would only mumble snatches of verse.

Ian knew that each of them was being judged and weighed for the slaughter. He knew that for the moment Smith was using them as a means of entertainment, a way of looking into the past. But that would soon change, he was sure of it.

They came for Ian while the others were asleep, and he quietly slipped away, not wishing to create another emotional scene. Smith was waiting for him in the same chamber but led Ian away through a side corridor and up into the docking bays. Not a single person did they meet, and Ian finally asked why.

"This whole unit is a shrine. If the ship of Columbus could be found, do you think we would sail it and use it? The same is true of this vessel—this once-crowded penal colony. Only my priests and priestesses live here, to oversee my needs."

"Your priests and priestesses?" He knew the tone of disdain couldn't be concealed.

Smith looked at him and smiled. "Come and gaze upon my power."

Smith led the way to the zero-gravity docking section. Passing *Discovery*'s port, the two boarded a small vessel and strapped into side-by-side couches. Smith activated a command screen then quickly rattled off a statement into the console mike. The shuttlecraft was activated, and they were off.

"Voice-activated commands?" Ian asked, impressed with the technology.

"Yes, I was rather amazed at the primitive piloting systems of your own vessel."

They traced a parabolic arc away from the main ship, and as they came up on the opposite side of the vessel, Ian couldn't help but gasp in amazement. In the harsh blue-white light of Delta Sag, hundreds of ships hung suspended in high orbit like fiery diamonds of light.

"What was once above Earth at the height of her power in space pales to insignificance when compared to this. Gregor says that there are now over ten thousand home vessels, from small ones such as the relic I now live in to giants, one hundred and fifty kilometers in length. Most are in orbit around this once-dead airless planet, which is so rich in the resources that we desire.

"When we arrived here nearly three hundred years ago, there were but twenty-five thousand of us. We fashioned crude landing vessels for the surface below and finally managed to gain a toehold. Those were exciting times, Ian Lacklin. Heroic times. Within several years the first mass-drivers were throwing up desperately needed supplies of silicon, iron, hydrogen, and oxygen, locked beneath the surface. Then we built the skyhooks, the powersats, and the first new habitation units. That took us fifty years. And then I approved the growth. Yes, the growth, where a mother could have more than two children. I now encouraged my people to have as many as possible. Since that time we've doubled our population every eighteen years."

Ian tried some quick mental arithmetic but Smith had already guessed his goal.

"According to Gregor, there are over one billion people

living in space. If we continue for another two hundred years at this rate of growth, we'll have over a trillion souls. One trillion souls. And that small planet down below shall disappear from our insatiable need. Think of that, Ian Lacklin. One trillion souls."

There was a sudden connection, and Ian couldn't help but ask.

"Why do they call you the Father?"

"Ah, yes." He chuckled softly with an obvious note of pride. "Simple, Ian Lacklin. Of that first generation of growth, I was the father of at least one child from every mother."

Ian looked at him and couldn't help but smile.

"You from the Outside, you can smile in my presence, but not in front of the others. *That* could be deadly.

"I know what you're thinking, that it must have been a laborious task. Some were done in, how shall I say, 'the traditional way,' but the vast majority were performed through artificial techniques. Of the next generation the same was done again, and again thereafter and thereafter. The genealogies are watched of course and the males of my community sire children, as well, but ultimately they all trace themselves back to me. So you see, Ian Lacklin, by now all one billion alive today are my descendents in one degree or another. It's strange, Ian, to meet a man twice my age, bent over with time, and to realize that I am his father or grandfather. Soon for me, only a matter of months from now in my life span, there will be a trillion who are descendents from my loins."

He said it with the pride of a biblical patriarch. One billion to date, Ian thought.

"I almost had the same arrangement myself," Ian said matter of factly.

"Oh, what happened?"

"The details of the contract didn't work out." And he wouldn't say another word on the subject.

They sat in silence for several minutes and Ian hoped that Smith would be duly impressed by that little revelation about the IFF and that there would be no more questions in that vein.

So, they were all descendents of Smith. The sociological implications were fabulous, and he wished that Ellen was with them at this moment. Smith had taken the primitive concept of the clan, with its family bondings, and raised it to the level of an entire civilization. He was Adam incarnate, master of an entire star system—and how much of a master, Ian would soon see.

Ian watched as Smith guided them on their trajectory toward one end of a cylinder that must have been a hundred kilometers in length.

Smith called out several approach commands and their shuttle swung in on the final run that was only a couple of hundred meters above a rotating surface so big that Ian felt he was orbiting a planet. His curiosity was aroused as to the mass of this ship and the gravitational field that it created.

As they approached the end of the cylinder, the shuttlecraft started to decelerate and Ian was surprised at the sudden realization that Smith's people had mastered inertia dampening for a sublight vessel.

Clearing the end of the man-made planet, the shuttle finally docked at the very center, in the zero-gravity area.

"This will only take a couple of minutes. Would you care to come along?"

How could he refuse? Ian eagerly followed behind Smith.

Their docking port was devoid of people, and it seemed to be encased, floors, walls, and ceilings, in gold. They floated into a small golden room with a single circular doorway at the other end.

"I shall go first, of course," Smith said. "I'd appreciate it if you would stay behind me. If you should drift alongside of me or in front of me, I'm afraid that wouldn't follow protocol at all. I'd be forced to kill you." He smiled. "Do we understand each other?"

Ian nodded.

"Good then." Smith pushed off and floated toward the door. At his approach it slid open, a sudden roar engulfed them, as if a storm-tossed sea was breaking outside the golden room.

Smith grabbed hold of a circular railing of gold, stopping his forward momentum. He stood there surrounded by thunder.

Ian cautiously slipped up to the doorway and peaked out. "My God, it's full of people," he whispered.

He was looking out into a vast cylinder-shaped audience chamber: a kilometer or more in diameter, its length ten kilometers back up into the vessel. The entire population of the one habitat—millions of them—had gathered in this one place.

"O my children," Smith shouted, and his amplified voice rose above the thunderous roar.

"For you are the Father of us all!" ten millions answered in return.

"Our promise shall be fulfilled, our glory magnified a thousandfold. Our revenge shall be just."

"For so you have promised!"

"Our Hegira shall come to an end in the gardens of Paradise!"

Smith reached to his belt and with a dramatic flourish drew a sword that glinted in the harsh blue sunlight pouring in through the windows that surrounded the docking port like a beaded halo.

Ian gasped with amazement as, like a field of steely wheat, a wavering shimmer of metal rippled up over the multitude. Until all human forms were blotted out beneath ten million upraised swords.

"Father, Father, Father . . ."

Smith pushed off from the golden ring and reentered the golden room.

"That is power, Ian Lacklin," he said with a cold glimmer of menace. "Think of that power when, in vengeance for what we suffered, I unleash it across the world that so cruelly drove us out into the night."

Ian was silent as together they reboarded the shuttle.

CHAPTER 14

Not a word was said between the two as the same performance was repeated at half a dozen other colonies.

Ian knew he had been invited to the ritual display to be impressed. But for what purpose? Part of it, he guessed, was to judge his reaction. But by the informal way that he was treated, Ian suspected that Smith was looking for a contact that was not filled with ritual, nor blood kin, for that matter.

Finally a question almost anthropological in nature broke the silence.

"Why the swords? I mean, I've been observing your technological level and it's simply astounding. Why this anachronism? Now, don't take offense, but in my eyes swords are rather ridiculous in a technological level anywhere beyond the Napoleonic. It's even stranger when I can't trace any useful cultural lineage out of it. I mean, swords were never used in space in your time, at least, not in anything above a poorly written video thriller."

"But there is a cultural lineage," Smith replied. "There's a direct historical linkage that centers our society around the sword and the mystique of the warrior. One more stop, Ian Lacklin, and then I shall explain."

The adulation seemed to have put Franklin Smith in a jovial mood, and he laughed as he entered through the airlock into yet another golden room. Ian sat in the shuttle and waited as the waves of noise washed the interior. For several minutes he looked across the star-studded night, the familiar formations now changed, with some brighter, and others dimmed, or lost altogether. Finally he found the one he was looking for, almost lost in the harsh glare of Delta.

The chanting would soon be heard there, as well, Ian realized, and he, more than anyone else alive, would be the one responsible for the devastation to come. He, a historian, a studier of others, a bookworm lost in fantasies of the heroic past would be the cause. Ian suddenly realized that in this movement he might very well be the prime ingredient in the fate of an entire world.

As his eyes scanned the shuttle, Ian recognized the superior technology. Hell, they had a thousand-year head start, a thousand years without the long night, the plagues, the convulsive wars that followed. Only in the last two hundred years had Earth reemerged into the enlightenment. For all practical purposes the only technological advantage his people had was the translight capability. In all others, they were sadly lacking. So now, thanks to his damnable curiosity, Earth's one small advantage would allow Smith to cross space in a matter of months—bringing with him the fire and sword of vengeance.

The chants were still thundering as Smith slipped into the seat next to him, closed the airlocks, and broke free and away.

"The day we left Earth orbit," Smith suddenly stated, picking up on a question that Ian had already half forgotten, "we numbered just over one hundred thousand.

The bastards who started the wars knew that we were trapped—we who were on that colony. Even if we made the engines, produced the sails, or deployed our ion packs, we were still trapped."

"Why?"

"Because the Earthside government forced one hundred thousand people aboard a colony designed for twenty-five thousand. It was such a crude analogy. Earth with her twelve billion had exceeded her carrying capacity, and those of us who protested and tried to alter that equation without resorting to war were forced onto a colony that had far exceeded *its* closed eco-capacity, as well. They knew we could only stay alive through massive trans-shipments from Earth. Those bastards reasoned that if they were defeated, they could still destroy us outright or leave us in space to linger a slow death until we finally destroyed ourselves.

"I remember one of their leaders laughing at me when we had just reached solar system escape velocity. He said he would enjoy contemplating the ways that we would use to kill each other."

Smith stopped for a moment and looked straight in the direction of Sol and the Earth that he had escaped.

"I outlived you, you bastards!" Smith screamed. "You laughed at me and I beat you all. And I'll be back with billions to seek revenge."

"The sword," Ian asked, trying to divert Smith away from what appeared to be a potentially violent tirade.

"Yes, the sword, your question about the sword," Smith replied absently.

He looked off into space, as if searching for some distant, painful memory. "Consider this problem, Ian Lacklin. You are acknowledged as the great leader of a group. Be it through cunning, political stealth, charismatic awe, or, in the very rare case, through actual ability to rule. You have a closed system, there are one hundred thousand people and you know that only twenty-five thousand will live. And you, Ian Lacklin, you alone can choose. What now would you do?"

Ian recoiled at the thought of the few possibilities. The harming of an insect was to him a moral question, and often he would catch a fly only to release it outside rather than kill it. True, he had played absurd "survival in the shelter" games while in graduate school, but this was different. The man before him was real and had faced that actual question—and had apparently solved it.

"I think I would have resigned or killed myself."

"Bullshit!" Smith thundered his response with such rage that Ian pulled back from him. "You sit here in your complacency and talk philosophical bullshit. First you absolve yourself of the problem, thereby attempting to make yourself morally superior. I hold such people in contempt. Complete contempt!"

"I'm not trying to show myself superior to you," Ian shouted back. "It's just that my mind rebels at finding a way to kill seventy-five thousand people."

Smith looked at Ian for a moment then smiled a sad, almost whimsical smile. "If any of my people had ever dared to speak to me like that, my followers would tear him apart. You know, I miss this. I truly miss this." He sighed and looked off into space for a moment. "Too bad it will have to end sometime.

"I still hold the moral whiners in contempt," Smith said, drawing the conversation back to its original path, "for they present an argument, such as nonviolence or disarmament and peace, while living in the safety of their sheltered lives. Let them truly be placed on the line, let them see their children starving in the name of peace, let them see their families bombed and raped—then see how their moral arguments stand.

"I think, Ian Lacklin, my pudgy, bespectacled, bookish professor, I think that if you were suddenly in the same situation as I . . ." His voice trailed away for a moment, as if the images he was arguing over were wavering before him like phantoms. "I think, Ian, that you, too, would finally learn to decide the fate of tens of thousands. Learn, at last, just how easy it really is. But back to the answer of your question, my friend."

He spoke a couple of quick commands into the nav system and the shuttle rolled into a different trajectory, aiming itself toward a close sweep of the small planet that was the source of Franklin Smith's strength. Then he turned back to their conversation.

"In short, Ian Lacklin, I had to devise a way to kill seventy-five thousand of my own people, otherwise all of us would die. Our council thought of raiding another colony, but we had yet to build the necessary weapons, and anyhow, the colonies were already destroyed in the opening stages of the war or far ahead of us on their trajectories.

"So we had to take in the following considerations before cutting back on our population. Our ecosystem was susceptible to sabotage; a small group of malcontents could seize a key point—the reactor, the central control system, or one of a hundred other points—and thereby blackmail the rest. Therefore I was forced to move swiftly and to create a state of tight control. It had to be harsh, ruthless, and unswerving in loyalty; and most important, instantaneous to command without thought of personal self.

"I realized, Ian, that a system employing Bushido was the key."

"Bushido?"

"An ancient word. Japanese, meaning a code of warriors' honor. It suited my needs perfectly. A system of feudal overlords with retainers who valued honor more than life; service to their clan's lord became the definition of their life. In short, Ian, it became the only way. I needed to instill discipline and an acceptance of death to serve the greater whole—a society where death was acceptable."

He fell silent for a moment and looked away. And Ian noticed a tremor in his jaw, as if he was fighting for control.

"I had to kill seventy-five thousand so twenty-five thousand could live," he whispered. "And there was no escaping that trauma. No escape for Dr. Franklin Smith, professor of philosophy from Berkeley.

"Our governmental system had been democratic, but the ruling body of our unit came to me, knowing what had to be done. They knew a democratic system would deadlock over the question of who would die. They feared some of the malcontents' taking over, and knowing that I was the pacifist and philosopher, they felt comfortable with my becoming the Angel of Death. Oh, they could wash their hands of it then—the stigma would be carried by Smith. Let Smith kill them; afterward we'll deal with him. I begged them at first not to nominate me, but in the end I took the position."

"What did you do then?" Ian asked, realizing why it was that Smith had spared him. Ian was the cathartic, the only one in Smith's universe that he could unburden to. He had for the moment become, like of old, the confessor to a Pope, the confessor to a god.

"I was married, you know," Smith replied, his voice barely a whisper. "Janet . . . Janet. I told her why and she understood. Then I killed her."

He looked away again and started to sob. The planet was rolling by beneath them, the shuttlecraft skimming a thousand meters above the surface. Pits the size of cities dotted the landscape, and from them rose streams of payloads propelled upward by the mass-drivers. As they approached the equatorial band, it seemed as if the planet were rimmed with the spokes of a wheel soaring upward to the geosync points, where processing plants manufactured the needs of a billion people. Ian didn't say a word as the quiet sobs filled the shuttle. Suddenly Smith stiffened and with a forceful effort turned and looked back at Ian.

"With that one death I gained the understanding and, thereby, the control over the others; they listened to one who had made the penultimate sacrifice. First, I ordered that the best and the brightest would be saved. Those with the superior intellect and the superior genetic capabilities would live to breed a superior race. They were isolated in a secure portion of the colony. The single doorway into that section became known as the Portal of Life, for only those chosen could go through it.

"Next I selected those with unique skills and knowledge who had not earlier been selected. I now had half the people that I could save."

"What did the council say to this plan?"

Smith's expression hardened. "They said nothing. After I killed Janet, my first order had been to kill every member of the council. They gave me the power—I used it. I killed them, for they all deserved to die. They would have used me in the end as their scapegoat, their Judas, and turned against me. For I realized that only by yielding to the decisions of a wise clan lord could we survive, and I would become that lord. I had already selected my bodyguards, those who would be my first generation of priests, though I knew that my cult would have to be developed gradually.

"I then created the Order of the Sword, and the system to exercise it. Hardly anyone had experience with sword work. It was fair, and simple. Our stores of steel were adequate and we manufactured those first weapons easily enough. Crude, they were, but sufficient. And thus for six months, day by day, the fighting of pairs became the path out. And with it, the forcing of obedience to my will, since those who were the best, those who could take the discipline, gradually became my closest guards and carriers of my will."

He chuckled with a deep solemn tone, which Ian found to be strange after the emotional outbreak of earlier.

"Human nature . . . so strange, so strange. They came to enjoy it, this warriors' code. The women became the fiercest at times, especially those who had lost children. Don't look at me that way, Ian, you must have known that when we were exiled we brought our families and children with us. It was a penal *colony*."

"What happened to the children?"

"Those with superior abilities were sent to the isolation area until the trials by arms were over. Those over twelve who did not make it that way had to fight. Those under twelve . . . we put to sleep."

"The children?"

"Don't call upon your moral superiority with me, Ian. If we had left them back on your Earth, they would have been vaporized in the war. Is that superior?"

Ian didn't particularly care for the way he said "your Earth," but he thought it best not to argue the point.

"But all those thousands who missed being defined as superior by only a small fraction, or by several points in the tests you once used. Would it not have been wise to try to save them? What about the brutes, the savage animals who would survive by killing, were they worth saving?"

"If I had not let them think they had a fair chance, they would have overthrown my plan. Can't you see the beauty of it? I let them think that they had the advantage. However, it was so simple. I matched brutals against brutals. Those who might oppose me against those who might oppose me. And those who might be worth saving, I tried, when possible, to match them against weaker opponents who were not worth saving but whom I could not simply execute.

"Through the fights it was so easy to deceive them and to keep them from destroying all of us in a mad frenzy of destruction, as the scum back on Earth had prophesied.

"And so for six long and bloody months, I reduced us step by step. The bodies were processed for their valuable resources, my people learned a new code, and we were transformed. And as I watched the Earth disappear astern, fading to a blue speck lost in the glare of a minor sun, I learned control.

"For they had destroyed Paradise!" He shouted the words, and Ian was tempted to tell him that he was not preaching to the multitude, but thought better of it.

"We saw what was coming, we had spoken out against it, and for our effort those fools had us exiled. I learned, Ian Lacklin, what is the nature of power. I could hop to one of my colonies right now, command ten thousand to kill themselves, and they would do so without question and consider it an honor. That, Ian Lacklin, is power— and it rests in my hands.

"Never again shall I ever let happen what those on Earth forced us to do."

They finally swung in to the dark side of the planet, and its surface was banded by necklaces of lighting that illuminated the planet as if it were day. Ian was amazed at the power being harnessed there. Smith's people were literally tearing the planet apart. As if reading his thoughts, Smith suddenly spoke again.

"Gregor gave me a report on our progress before you joined me. He said that it was recently calculated that if growth continues at its current rate, we will totally consume the mass of that planet in four hundred years. Already we are developing five of the moons on the first gas giant."

"Which one is that?"

"It's called Janet."

"Of course." Ian said it with such understanding that Smith suddenly reached out and touched him on the arm and smiled briefly.

"But as I was saying, I saw the path. Once the Time of Blooding had finished, I realized that the warrior code must stay. So with the coming of the next generation, I encouraged its development along with rigorous training of the mind and total discipline. Ian, I knew that the odds were still against us. I had set a course that would take seven hundred years—fearing that if we went to the closer stars, we would find ourselves in competition. I knew many were bound for the galactic core, but space is immense. We had contact with several colonies on the way out, but most we would not reach. Two did make starfall here at Delta Sag and we were forced to deal with them, since of course they were not of us."

"I know. I found the results of your actions."

Smith ignored his comment and continued.

"I created a warrior-guard elite, and I acted as a guide to the future so that there would be a continuity with the past. As least, that is what I told them, but I knew what would happen after only several generations.

"I was awakened every twenty years, or when there was a crisis to advise—to give counsel and to plan. The first time I was greeted like an old friend returning. The second time only a few from the 'Earth Time,' as they were calling it, still remembered me. And on the fourth time, there was not one in fifty. And I started to become first an advisor, then a legend, and finally a god—as I knew I would."

He smiled at Ian as he said the words, and a man who had sounded before to be so sane now took on a different edge, his powerful appearance and deep rich voice lending only more power to the image of something almost superhuman.

"My awakening became a religious event, a long-cherished high holy day by which people measured their lives. When I knew the time to be right, I laid out the next step—the bonding of all by one common blood. It became a most sacred privilege to bear my child, even if induced artificially. And it became the most cherished dream of a maiden to surrender her virginity to me and then to bear my child." Smith looked at Ian and gave a slightly lascivious smile.

"It was easy to keep track of the genetics of it, and within a few hundred years every single person became a descendent of myself. I am, therefore, truly the Father of all my people!"

He shouted out the words and laughed as he did so, and then fixed Ian with his gaze.

"And I knew one other part of the formula that was necessary for our health and survival. A people must always have a dream. And I gave them the dream. That we would increase in number and then return one day to the paradise that had been fouled by those who are not of our blood. They would return to the promised land, led by their Father—and we would purge the Earth of its filth. We would take our revenge for having been driven out. We would take our revenge for the Blooding Time. And we would then dwell in the realm of Paradise forever!"

Smith grabbed Ian's arm with such force that Ian feared the madman's grip would burst right through his skin and shatter the bone beneath.

"And you, Ian Lacklin, you gave me the means of my return. Your people are weak, your own ship's computer tells me you number not half a billion on the entire planet. You have but a weak central government controlled by an overgrown bureaucracy. There is no way that you can defy me. We have searched to transcend light for a millennium, and to think that its discovery would be a mere accident by an amateur back on Earth. But now I know. I have the data in your machine to tell me how. And then I shall return in glory and my people can at last return to Paradise!"

CHAPTER 15

IAN FELT A MOMENT OF DISORIENTATION. THE DARKNESS WAS strange. Shortly after his return from his meeting, a meal had been delivered that outshone anything they had experienced since Earth. In spite of the circumstances, Ian was enthralled with the dinner plates; each was stamped "Souvenir of the 2064 New York World's Fair." Ian slipped one of the coffee saucers into his jacket pocket. It now rested next to the alien artifact.

It had already occurred to the crew of *Discovery* that this was to be some sort of ceremonial last supper—and they were suddenly convinced of it when the lights were dimmed. Nervously they sat together until eventually exhaustion and the need for a final private moment had sent them to their own small areas.

As if stirred by a distant voice, Ian awoke from his sleep and looked toward the doorway. A shadow filled the dimly lit corridor—Smith. Leaving the others to what he feared might be a final rest, Ian stood and followed Smith to the audience chamber.

"Have you decided?"

"First, I give you permission to sit." And Smith beckoned for him to sit on the small stool placed before the dais.

Smith was dressed in the flowing ceremonial robes of the warrior, his sword resting on the floor by his right hand. The soft lamplight behind him haloed his salt-and-pepper hair and cast darkened shadows that hid his beard and ebony features.

Ian gave him a nod of thanks and settled down onto the stool. Smith said nothing, and Ian finally broke the silence.

"I can't understand one thing."

"Go on."

Ian drew in his breath and finally committed himself. "You have the information that you need from us. We therefore serve no logical purpose by living. You, if anyone, have learned to kill without prejudice or sentiment. If we do not serve a purpose, then why don't you kill us?"

Smith leaned forward and his features emerged from the shadows. "You are correct, Ian Lacklin. You've surmised that you still serve a purpose, and now you ask me what it is."

"Yes."

Smith chuckled softly. "Are the universities still the same as when I was there?"

The change of tack threw Ian off balance for a second, but he quickly picked up on it. "I have a feeling that it's universal and timeless."

"Still the same administrators?" He chuckled softly. "You know, I could never figure out how people so dumb and so deceitful ever got into education."

Ian nodded and found himself chuckling, as well.

"And still the same dumb jocks who your dean forces you to pass, in spite of their idiocy?"

"I think I know what jock means, we call them ozone heads. But yes—it is still the same. Most schools are still places were education is second to the god of sports."

"It's just that I was once a full professor of philosophy," Smith said sadly, "and I know that you were a professor of history, specializing in my time."

"I thought that was part of the reason you kept my friends and me alive."

"But events, Ian Lacklin, will soon force the end of this nostalgic interlude. I was a professor, but now I am something entirely different."

Ian found it remarkable that he was gripped by an icy feeling of calm. The path was open to him. He could sense it in Smith's words. The reason he had not heard from Smith or, for that matter, the reason they had not yet been eliminated was simply because Smith was not sure of the path to follow. Smith as the Angel of Death was poised, but something behind him held him back. Ian now knew that it rested with him—an overweight, nearsighted, certifiably incompetent history teacher—to talk the man out of slaughtering the entire population of the Earth, or he would die trying.

He thought about that for a moment. He could die as soon as the session was over. To his surprise his bowels didn't turn to water, and his knees didn't quake at the mere thought of it all. His arguments were already forming, and he started.

"I guess it's obvious that you intend to use the plans for our faster-than-light vessel. You'll build a fleet and in short order return to Earth."

Smith smiled softly and nodded.

"With fire and sword," his deep voice boomed, "as they say."

Ian took a deep breath. "You're a fool!" His voice

echoed in the chamber. And for a moment there was a look of shock on the face of Smith.

The sword seemed almost to leap into Smith's hand and arc back in a sweep that would culminate in death. Ian steeled himself for the numbing blow and stilled the terror in his heart. He looked into Smith's eyes and held him with a challenge.

Smith held his gaze, and wild desire was mirrored in his eyes, as if he wrestled with himself. Ian waited, amazed at the sudden intensity of reality and thought that held him. It was as if in a single second he could clearly consider a dozen different thoughts. He was amazed at the almost ludicrous realization that he was engaged in a diplomacy that the world might never know of. He was amazed, as well, at the cold-blooded logic that had driven him to insult Smith.

And Ian Lacklin felt a secret pride. He had, for one moment, at least, transcended; and as an old word had described, he was no longer a wimp. Ian Lacklin had equaled, at last, his fabled heroes of old.

Smith kept the sword poised, and then with a sudden flourish he drove it into the flooring by his side and released it—so that the handle quivered and swayed as if it held a trembling life of its own.

"Explain!" Smith barked. And shaking with suppressed emotion, he turned away.

"There is no need for me to be pedantic, your education is better than mine. And as is so very rare, you do not let that education hamper you with useless rhetoric. You therefore understand the nature of societal movements. That has been my career. I studied your movements, your age.

"A society must have a tangible goal, a utopian dream of what it can transcend to. It can be, as in the Middle Ages, a drive to religious oneness and establishment of the kingdom of God. To my own ancestors it was an all-consuming passion to transcend the near-fatal damage of the Holocaust and return us to space. For you it is revenge."

"Yes, revenge!" Smith shouted. "You were not there. I was. I saw the light slip out of Janet's eyes, I saw the bloodied floor of the fighting pits, I carry the blood of the tens of thousands on my soul. And I saw what they did on Earth. They did it! They did it!" His voice rose to a scream of rage.

"They are dead a thousand years," Ian whispered in reply. "Franklin Smith, you are nearly the last of your age; you dream a revenge against those who are dust, their legacies forgotten, their age destroyed in a Holocaust of their own making. Damn it, Smith, they're nothing except your memory."

He fell silent, waiting for the reply, but there was no response. And Smith still kept his back to him. Ian searched for the historical example.

"Your logic is the same as if the blacks of your age were to punish the whites of your South for an experience gone two hundred years, or a Jew of my time to punish what were once Germans for that first Holocaust more than a millennium ago."

"But the memories are still here and alive." Smith turned and pointed to his heart. "Still alive and burning in here."

"You've had revenge enough, Franklin Smith, revenge enough. That traveler of mine, Elijah, he said 'For I alone have lived to tell thee this tale.' You know, you murdered his entire colony. That poor mad fool quoting ancient literature is all that is left of an entire world, and that is your work."

"It was necessary."

"So was what happened to you."

Smith's hand rested again on the sword.

"Go ahead, if that's your answer to what might save you, then go ahead and get it over with. I'm tired of waiting for it."

"Speak then, damn you."

"The world was tottering toward madness. To an insane world the voice of sanity is usually viewed as insane. You're lucky they didn't kill you on the spot. At least *you* had a chance. You're no better than they are, for you'd have done the same. In fact you have done the same in the name of saving your society.

"Think of it, Smith. The madness that seized the world forced over seven hundred colonies and nearly thirty million people to flee the Earth. It was violent, in many cases nearly hopeless, and millions died. But the bonds had been broken. Right now hundreds of civilizations are spreading slowly across this area of the galaxy. The birth of a child is attended by blood and trauma. So, too, usually with a civilization. That madness, that trauma forced you to flee and, yes, forced the tragedy of your life. But I see here a billion people, bonded together in a new civilization that you have forged out of your own power and desire. That has only happened to a handful of men in history. You are the Adam, Abraham, and Moses of a new civilization."

"And now the angel of war," Smith replied.

"Death, you mean. And as I said before, you'd be a fool."

"You're just arguing to save your own life and your own world."

"Of course I am. Only a madman desires death. Only a madman desires his world to die. But I see the death of all in this; your world and mine will die."

"How so? I've looked at your records; I know your capabilities. In ten years I could destroy you completely. Even if your people learned of my coming, still I would overwhelm them."

"Yes, even if my people knew. You already outnumber us nearly four to one, and in ten years time it will be six to one. Your technology is generations beyond our own, all except for that one small quirk of fate that caused one of our people to discover the way of circumventing light-speed. That is our only superiority, and you now have that, as well.

"But I tell you this, Franklin Smith. Lead your people for a revenge that only you need have, and it will destroy you and your civilization in the process."

"Give me your argument then, and be done with it. I am growing weary of this talk."

"My opening argument is that a civilization needs a goal. You've set up the goal for your people: the desire for revenge. You've created a perfect machine for that goal: a billion people linked together by common blood, a people trained in what you called Bushido, and a technological level that transcends Earth's—as if your twenty-first-century world had found a way to wage war on a rabble of medieval knights.

"But remember that concept about a goal. So you go ahead, you build and then you attack. You use atomics to blast us and sweep life off the face of the Earth. You have triumphed, Franklin Smith. Imagine that triumph."

He looked into Smith's eyes expecting the vision he painted to be one that would excite, but to his surprise there was nothing, as if Smith could already see the path that Ian was pointing to.

"And then what? Damn it, tell me, then what? You've selected a goal that can be too easily reached. Oh, it was a wonderful goal that could bind a people together when they needed binding. You engineered that superbly well. But now, thanks to me, you can attain that goal. Once you've reached it, however, what can revenge bring?"

"It can still bring a payment here," Smith replied, striking his chest. "Here it will bring a rich reward."

"A reward of the moment. But a societal revenge, once it is reached, bears a strange price. Once the goal has been obtained, then there is no goal—no dream to reach out to. Nothing now to work toward. And then the old prophets and the old dreams are cast aside. Think, man, of the contempt your age felt for the century-long quest for revenge in the Middle East. They had their revenge and destroyed their foe, taking back what they called the usurped lands, and think in the end of the bitter retribution that came—and how it was created by themselves."

To his surprise Smith nodded his head in response. "I lost several classmates in that war, I remember now."

"I could argue this point for hours, Franklin Smith, but that is foolish. You're the philosophy professor, you should be able to follow the argument on your own. I am merely the historical observer.

"If your society reaches its goal, then it will change forever—and in a direction you might not have anticipated or be able to control. The very factors that bind it together, that give it strength and vitality, will be lost. Your own America was built on a goal of expansion and limitless opportunity. When you started to listen to the drivel of idiots who said there must be limits to growth and that expansion into space is wrong, you fell behind. It was nearly fatal, for the Japanese and Chinese never had such doubts.

"Go ahead and make your goal. They'll throw you aside then, Smith. You've already started toward another goal; if you point that way, you can't lose."

"Go ahead," Smith replied sarcastically, "enlighten me, Professor."

"The complete settling of space is the only goal that can be sought and yet, ultimately, never obtained. With the hibernation drug you could take your people in that direction for ten thousand more years. At your rate of growth you could be tens of trillions, reaching out across the entire galaxy. That's a hell of an alternative. Don't go back to Earth, Smith. Go ahead and kill us if need be, but don't go back to Earth. Revenge isn't worth the cost. You shaped a destiny for your people, continue to do it. In five or six generations your people could forget that the hatred of Earth ever existed—and the dream could be redirected elsewhere."

"But you Earthmen could one day be a threat."

"That's like saying a Carthaginian army could have threatened the America of your twenty-first-century. Damn it, Smith, you've got such an exponential jump on Earth, it'll never catch up. Besides, our society is still primarily planetbound. We've learned; our society's ethic limits population growth. Less than one-tenth of one percent of us are space dwellers, and the vast majority of those out there still look back down to Earth. We're a people who've learned to live within our ecosystem, as those aboard any space colony must do. It's pretty boring in a way, but that's the way I guess we'll always be. We cast off our seed, and some of us will still go out, but the grim necessities of it have already been done by our ancestors.

"But *your* people, *your* vibrant society is not looking inward, dependent on a single planet. Your people are already looking out toward the rest of the universe. The hell with Earth, Franklin Smith, you've got an entire universe to populate with your descendents."

Ian fell silent. And for several minutes nothing more was said.

"You know something, Ian, you are neither as dumb nor as wimpish as I first thought. Your argument is sound and bears thinking. After all, the distant future is only a matter of months for me, but generations for my people. We have a significant lead on you already, and now, with this light drive, there is nothing to fear from your people."

Smith stretched and walked over to rest his hand on the hilt of the sword. "However, Ian Lacklin, though it saddens me to say this, I think you should pray to whatever god it is that you worship, for it is time that you meet him."

"Wait a minute, Doc," Ian said hurriedly, coming to his feet, "I thought that you'd see we weren't a threat, I mean, you know . . ."

Smith drew the blade out of the floor and advanced on Ian.

"Look at it from my perspective, Ian, and try to be reasonable. I still have a touch of the paranoid in me. If I let you go there is the slim chance that you could create quite a problem for me some day. Besides, I have the designs for your ship, so there's no need to let others know that I have it. Therefore . . ." He shrugged his shoulders and grimaced as if he were being forced into an unpleasant act.

"You ask me to be reasonable?" Ian shouted. "Damn it, you're going to cut my head off and you want me to be reasonable!"

"I'm sorry, Ian, I *do* like you. I promise your passing will be quick and painless. Now just kneel down so I won't miss my aim and cause you undue suffering."

"Bullshit! I've tried to be reasonable, but you wouldn't listen. So you've forced me into it." Ian reached into his pocket.

"Come along now, Ian, we searched you for weapons, and I was good enough to allow you to keep your personal effects. Now don't try to threaten me."

"I'm not threatening you," Ian said coldly. "There's a thermonuclear mine aboard our ship; your sensing devices should have picked up the radiation signature."

"So what?"

Ian pulled the alien cylinder out of his pocket. "This is the trigger."

"Come on, Ian Lacklin, you're bluffing. That's a useless piece of junk."

"I thought so, too. But it's a small, alien transmitting device. Just before we jumped to this region I rigged it up to trigger the mine."

Smith was silent, watching Lacklin's eyes for some telltale clue.

Ian was actually shaking. "I'm not joking this time,

Smith. I didn't want this situation, I had hoped we could get along without threats, but you forced me into this."

Ian held the cylinder over his head and touched the end of it with his thumb.

"Take another step and you'll get to see firsthand what real eternity is all about. All I need to do is push down on the end of this cylinder and *puff*, you and I will be gamma rays."

Ian was staring straight into Smith's eyes and a taunting smile crossed his face. He was in control!

"I'll tell you something, Smith," Ian said, his voice reflecting his sense of assurance. "I've listened to you for some time now, in fact, I've even grown to like you, but the game is over. So here's what you're going to do for me. First off, you're going to call the guards off my friends, and then we'll take a nice leisurely stroll down to the docking ports."

"And if I refuse?"

"Then we'll see right now if I'm bluffing or not."

Smith still held him with his gaze, but Ian knew he had the upper hand.

"Look, Smith, we pose no threat, we only stir a fear that should have been buried a millennium ago. Now if I push this button you die, and when you go the civilization that is built around your semigodhood dies with you. Logic therefore dictates that we take that little walk to the docking bay. You can save face by making sure all your people are ordered from the area. Later just tell them that you decided to let us live. So you win. And even if I'm bluffing, you'd still win anyhow; we and the Earth pose no threat to you."

Smith started to smile but Ian's gaze held steady as he started to move his thumb.

"Stasz, is all secure in there?"

"Engines are powering up, Ian. All secured, just tell

me when to close the airlock and let's get the hell out of here."

Ian switched off the comlink and looked at Smith, who floated on the other side of the airlock.

"So, what are you waiting for, Ian? I've done as you requested, I've let you and the others return to your ship. So go on, get the hell out of here."

"Do you think I'm that dumb?" Ian said, edging his voice with contempt.

Smith's knuckles whitened as he clenched his hands. "Don't push it, Lacklin. You're aboard your ship, now just get the hell out of here."

"Before we can jump to light you could vaporize us with your ship's defenses, or the defenses of any one of a hundred of your other ships."

Smith smiled.

"Checkmate. I could force you to come with us," Ian said.

"Then I'd call your bluff. You'll not take me off this ship to suffer the humiliation of being held hostage."

"Checkmate," Ian replied sadly. Ian drew a deep breath and stepped out of the airlock. There was no other way and he had assumed from the beginning that it would end like this. He held Smith in control only as long as the threat was in front of him.

"Stasz, listen to me."

"Go ahead, boss."

Boss, Stasz had just called him boss! "Stasz, I want you to remove the thermomine from the aft storage area and bring it to me in the airlock."

Smith's eyes grew wider and Ian held the cylinder up as a warning not to try anything.

"Ian, what the hell are you doing?" Stasz replied.

"Don't argue with me on this. He'll vaporize us as soon as we pull out. I'm staying behind with the mine as a guarantee to make sure he doesn't. Now dump that mine and just get the hell out of here."

Afraid that Smith might try a desperate move, Ian held him with his gaze. "An even swap, Smith. They get away and I'll surrender the mine and this trigger, then you can do as you see fit."

A flicker of a smile crossed Smith's face.

"Most noble on your part, Doctor."

Ian felt the airlock open behind him.

"You sure you want to do this?" Stasz asked. Ian looked at him from the corner of his eye. Stasz was floating in the entryway, the ugly black mine tucked under his arm.

"Just toss it over here, get back on the controls and punch it the hell out of here."

"Ian?"

"Goddamm it, do it!" Ian shouted.

"Thanks for saving my retirement," Stasz said sadly, "I'll see they put your name on a gold plaque." And with a reluctant gesture Stasz gave the bomb an underhand toss.

"Ian, my love, you can't!"

With a wild shout Shelley barged past Stasz and ricocheted off a bulkhead, knocking the slowly tumbling bomb off course. She came straight at Ian, her arms outstretched like a distraught lover reaching for her mate.

She slammed into Ian even as the bomb drifted past him, just out of reach. He could see Smith leaping from the other side, grasping both for the bomb and the alien swizzle stick which had been knocked out of his hand by the impact of a sobbing Shelley.

"Shelley, let go!"

Floating in the zero gravity, the two men slammed into each other—each grappling for a hold.

"Really, Smith," Ian shouted, "two Ph.D.'s should find a better way to settle their disputes." He pulled back his right hand for a roundhouse punch.

Ian's entire body was thrown into the blow, and Ian was amazed to see blood spray even as he recoiled away.

He slammed up against the opposite wall to be met by a solid blow to his lower back. He had hit the mine, driving it into the wall and activating the last switch.

"Warning, warning, you have preactivated the Clearance Assured AB-23A thermomine. We are happy that you have decided to go with the best bang in the universe. And remember to contact our quality control people if you have any problem.

"Warning, Warning..."

The high-pitched voice, sounding like a video advertiser, droned on as Ian finally managed to grab a handhold and stopped his wild gyrations. Smith was dazed, and floated before him like a damaged ship that had lost all power to move or react.

"Ian, let's go!" Shelley's hands were yanking on his leg; a sudden tug pulled him back toward the airlock.

She pulled him through the airlock door and hit a button on the control panel; the door slammed shut.

"Stasz, punch us the hell out of here," Shelley screamed.

"The artifact," Ian shouted. "Wait, it's the only thing we have! I've got to go back."

Ian reached over to hit the airlock door release. There was a faint shudder as Stasz cut free from the docking port. Instantly the prejump acceleration kicked on, pushing Ian and Shelley against the opposite wall.

Reaching out Smith snatched the slowly tumbling mine. Pushing off from the wall, he floated down the corridor and stopped at a viewing port.

They were already free and accelerating into their jump.

With his left hand Smith touched his nose and winced with pain.

Damn it, that little guy broke his nose.

But that little guy would be vapor in fairly short order.

He reached over to a comlink board and got ready to call in the command to activate a weapons battery. The mine kept shrieking out its warning and he suddenly realized that the last thing he needed was for that warning to be going on in the background. Some of his "priests" were feeling a little uppity this time around, the way he imagined the pope would feel if God showed up and tried to take over the business. The last thing he needed was for them to think there had been a screw up. First the mine, then a couple of disabling shots.

"Warning, warning . . ."

"All right, shut up, damn it."

He examined the six numbered levers that were now in the down position. Simple enough. He grabbed hold of the last one and flicked it up.

"Congratulations, you have activated the final trigger. If you wish to deactivate it, please check your service manual at once. To avoid accidents, be sure the manual is the correct one for your model," the voice said cheerfully. "We advise that you now leave the area. Ninety seconds, eighty-nine, eighty-eight . . ."

Smith let go of the mine and it hovered in front of him.

"Oh, shit."

CHAPTER 16

"EARTHBOUND, IAN?"

"How long would it take, Stasz?"

"Six months seventeen days."

Ian did a quick calculation. That would put them in ten days before registration for the fall semester. Perfect! He could throw together a syllabus and be ready to go. Hell, for that matter they might even want him at Nouveau Harvard after his exploits.

Ian looked around at the others. Smith's system was ten billion kilometers behind them and the initial euphoria over their escape was wearing off.

"What's wrong, Shelley? We could be back in time for fall classes."

"Ian, I just remembered something."

"Yeah, what?"

"Did you file for a waiver from the mandatory recertification seminar?"

"The what?"

"Every third year all professors have to be recertified with six credits of education courses. The seminar was scheduled for the month after we left. You had to file before we left."

"Damn it, Shelley, what are you talking about? Anyhow, you're my assistant, you should have taken care it."

"I tried to tell you before we left. You had to file at the Provincial Office in person, at the Dean of Education's office."

"Hell, Shelley, they should allow me the waiver now. I can claim life experience. Damn, with all the data I'm bringing back, I can finally get published! I might even make it on the late-night videos. That should be worth six lousy education credits."

"Sorry, Ian, this seminar was on proper use of forms and the motivation of athletics students. They won't let you get a waiver."

"What the hell do you mean!"

"Ian," Ellen interjected, "remember the Chancellor said we all had to follow proper channels."

"And I suppose you did."

"But of course," she said with a self-confident snicker.

"And you never bothered to remind me."

"You should know what's important in education. Your certification is your problem, not mine."

He could see the triumph in her eyes.

"Ian, I hate to interrupt, but I'm picking up a faint beacon. It's way the hell over toward the course for the galactic core, several light-years out. But damn, is it powerful to get this far!"

Stasz turned around in his seat and looked at Ian expectantly.

Ian looked at Richard, but he was already out of it. There was no sense in even asking Elijah.

He looked at Ellen and smiled.

"Well, Miss Certification, looks like you're going to miss the next semester, as well!"

"Ian, you wouldn't!"

"I can tell you one thing I've read the paperwork on. According to the grant, I'm in command of this ship so I need not be democratic."

He looked past Ellen and gave a command that he had long fantasized about. "Full speed ahead, Stasz."

"Oh, by the way, Ian," Richard said while stirring from his lethargic stupor, "can you explain what the hell this is? Shelley said she picked it up in the corridor while you and Smith were wrestling about in such a deplorable fashion. She gave it to me thinking it came from my late lamented drinking kit."

Richard held the alien artifact in his hand. Ian shot a quick look over to Elijah, who sat silent, as if the object were a mystery to him as well.

"Oh, it just fell out of my pocket," Ian responded lamely as he rushed over to grab the most valuable artifact known to Man.

"Curious looking." Richard held it up for everyone to see. "What the hell is this blue button for?"

"Don't!"

Too late! With an exclamation of pain Richard dropped the rod after a flicker of flame shot out the opposite end.

Ian picked it up and nervously pressed the blue button. An inch or so of bright blue flame shot out the opposite end.

"Ian, what the hell are you doing with a cigarette lighter?" Shelley asked. "You don't even smoke."

"Oh, just saving the Earth with it," Ian said evenly. He turned and walked out of the room.

A cigarette lighter, he had faked out the most powerful man in the universe with a goddamn alien cigarette lighter—and his laughter echoed through the ship.

Alone in the main cabin, he punched into the ship's computer and in fairly short order the first analysis came in on the beacon. It looked like L-5 *319*!

He remembered that one. Even as he started to call up the data he heard the scuffle of boots on the deck.

"Come on over, as long as it isn't Ellen."

He didn't look up. He was bent over the screen checking the data.

There was a faint smell of perfume. He looked around.

"Oh, hi, Shelley. This is going to be a good one. This is a unit I always wanted to meet. It's a bunch of Tolkien buffs. Know what that is? Why, they were people who loved a most interesting form of literature popular in the twentieth century. Say, Shelley . . . Shelley."

He turned around. Good lord, she was undressing right in front of him.

He tried to stammer a protest, but before he could form any words she had kicked aside the last of her clothing to reveal a tight teddy.

"Shelley, w-why don't we talk about *319?*" Ian stammered.

"Let's not, Dr. Lacklin," she said softly. And, reaching past him, she turned the machine off.

Ian thought about the flash they had seen just before jump out, and wondered if it had taken Smith.

But then Shelley managed to drive that thought away, as well. Suddenly he realized that exciting as the voyage had been so far, it was definitely going to get better.

ABOUT THE AUTHOR

William R. Forstchen, who makes his home in Oakland, Maine, was born in 1950. Educated by Benedictine monks, he considered the calling of the priesthood but decided instead to pursue a career in history. Completing his B.A. in education at Rider College, he went on to do graduate work in the field of counseling psychology.

William was a history teacher for eight years and currently devotes his time to writing, educational affairs and the promotion of the peaceful exploration of space. William lives with his wife, Marilyn, their dog, Ilya Murometz, and Tanya the cat.

He recently led a group of fifty high school students to the Soviet Union which presented a resolution passed by the Maine State Legislature calling for a Soviet/American manned mission to Mars.

William's interests include iceboating, Hobie Cat racing, sailing, skiing, pinball machines, Zen philosophy, and participation in Civil War battle reenactments as a private in the 20th Maine Volunteer Infantry.